CHICKEN PESTO MURDER

THE DARLING DELI SERIES, BOOK 5

PATTI BENNING

SUMMER PRESCOTT BOOKS PUBLISHING

CHAPTER ONE

Spring had well and truly sprung in the town of
Maple Creek. The small town, nestled on the west
coast of Michigan, was beginning to show signs of
life again, with tiny green buds on the trees, and
birdsong filling the air. Moira Darling took a deep
breath, looking up at the clear sky before turning
back to the delivery man. There was work to be
done.

"I can take it from here," she told him, nodding to
the boxes of fresh goods piled neatly just inside the
deli's side door. "Thanks for helping me bring the
boxes in. I'll see you next month."

Her goodbyes said, the owner of Darling's DELI-
cious Delights slipped back inside the building and

shut the door firmly behind her, pausing to double-check that it had locked shut before facing the boxes. Her hands on her hips, she considered the best assignment of tasks.

"How can I help, Ms. D?" Darrin, the lanky young man that had been working for the deli since it opened, poked his head through the door that led to the main part of the deli.

"Do you think you could take care of the dry goods? I'll handle the perishable items. I've been meaning to clean out the freezer again anyway."

"Sure thing." He disappeared for a second—probably to tell Dante that he was on his own with the register—then strode into the kitchen, washed his hands, and grabbed a box cutter. "Let's get to work."

It didn't take them long to get everything put away. Moira kept the kitchen well organized; everything had a place, and she knew exactly where those places were. The deli was her pride and joy, and she spent nearly as much time there as she did at her house. The kitchen, with stainless steel appliances, a gas range, and the six-foot-deep walk-in pantry, was like a second home to her.

"There's someone at the register that wants to talk to you," Dante, her other male employee, said as he walked into the kitchen. "I came back here to see if I could help Darrin while you're up front, but it looks like you two handled unpacking everything already."

"We're pros," she told him with a grin. "But feel free to help him break down the boxes. Put them in my car when you're done; I might as well reuse them when Candice moves later this summer."

"Will do, Ms. Darling," Dante said. Darrin gave her a thumbs up, and the two of them got to work on breaking down and folding the cardboard boxes that the food had come in.

She was surprised and a bit concerned when she saw Detective Jefferson waiting for her by the register. Had something bad happened? Her first concern was for her daughter, Candice, who had left a few hours ago to go shopping in the city.

"Is everything all right?" she asked him, unable to keep the worry out of her voice.

"Everything is fine," he assured her. "I'm not here for police business. Well, I sort of am. I'm sure you remember Detective Fitzgerald?"

She nodded. There was no way that she would forget the older, taciturn detective who had been on the force for as long as she could remember. She might not have the friendliest relationship with him, but she definitely respected him and his devotion to his work.

"He's retiring this month," Jefferson told her. "We're planning a party for him on his last day. It will be an open event, and I'm hoping that we'll have a good turnout. He's really helped a lot of people during his time as a detective. Would it be all right if I left this flyer in your window? It's got all the information for the party on it."

"Of course." She smiled. "And you can count on me to be there. Do you need catering or anything?" she offered. "I'd be more than happy to supply a platter of sandwiches, or a cheese and meat platter."

"That would be wonderful," he said, smiling. "Thanks for your support. I'm going to miss him. He was my mentor when I first started as a beat cop. I'm just glad that he's not planning on moving away. Our chief left for Florida when he retired."

"I hope he enjoys his retirement," she said. "I'm sure he deserves it."

After the detective left, she rejoined Dante and Darrin in the back to see how they were coming along with breaking down the boxes. She wasn't sure how many Candice would need when she moved. She wasn't even sure when her daughter would be *able* to move; she had been having trouble finding a good place to open up her business in Lake Marion, the next town over. Well, she *had* found a place, the perfect place, but the man who owned it had left town and his granddaughter, who ran the shop, hadn't been very helpful when they wanted to get in touch with him. For her daughter's sake, she hoped that the mess got figured out soon, though she couldn't help but be glad that Candice would be living with her for a little while longer.

Her daughter had only lived away from home for two out of her twenty years, and those had been two of the loneliest years of Moira's life. She had opened the deli during that time as a hobby. What might she do when Candice moved out for good? Maybe *she* should move to Florida and open some sort of shop there. She grinned to herself at the thought of herself in some seaside restaurant, serving up gator tail and shrimp instead of delicatessen-style soups and sandwiches. Somehow that just didn't seem like her. No, she would miss the sleepy little towns that dotted the coast of Lake Michigan. This was where she had grown up and raised her own daughter. She didn't plan on leaving it any time soon

"That's all of them, Ms. D," Darrin said as he came back to the counter from the kitchen.

"Thanks, you guys," she said.

"No problem." He and Dante traded a look, and Moira raised an eyebrow. They looked like they were planning something.

"What's going on?" she asked.

"Well, we were talking while we worked," Darrin began. "And I thought that since the deli has been doing so well lately, we might get even more customers if we extended the hours."

"I've actually been thinking of that, but I really don't want to be open much later than we are now. Things start to slow down the hour before we close anyway, and I don't think that enough people would come in for the extra hours we would all have to work to be worth it," she told him.

"We don't mean that we should stay open later in the evening," Dante chimed in. "But open earlier in the morning. I think a lot of people would come in if we offered some breakfast items."

"Now that's an idea," Moira said, her mind already racing. Right now, the deli opened for lunch and closed shortly after the dinner rush. Breakfast might bring a fair amount of new customers in. "We would have to figure out a breakfast menu," she added, thinking out loud. "And we would need a new supplier for eggs. We could start offering freshly squeezed juices; I've been meaning to buy a juicer anyway. The hours would be the most difficult thing to figure out. Would either of you be willing to work more?"

"Yes," they said together.

"Especially during the summer," Darrin added. "Since I won't have classes."

"And I can work as much as you want me to, Ms. Darling. Any extra hours are welcome," said Dante.

"I'll think about it," she promised them. "I definitely do want to expand, I'm just not quite sure how yet."

She had sent the two employees home and begun the task of cleaning up after a busy day when a familiar black car pulled into the parking lot. Moira smiled to herself when she saw David Morris get out of it and begin walking towards the deli's front door. The private investigator had helped her more times than she could count since she had met him a few months ago. Even though he lived in Lake Marion, which was a good half hour away, he still managed to find reasons to visit her at work a few days each week.

They had gone on a couple of dates since he had first asked her out just over a month ago; she was glad that none of them had turned out as disastrously as the first one. Moira enjoyed spending time with David, but she wished that she didn't have so much else going on at the same time. Between running the deli, helping Candice start her own business, and taking care of the house, she just didn't have time for much of a social life.

She unlocked the doors for him, and leaned her mop against the wall. The floor was already nearly sparkling, but there were a few stubborn scuff marks that didn't want to come off. If only she could afford to put new floors in, the place would look so much better.

"Hey," she greeted the private detective. "What brings you to town?"

"I was just driving through," he said. "I had to go to Wellsville for a case, and I decided to take the scenic route back."

"I'm glad you did," she replied with a grin. "It's always nice to see a friendly face. Do you want anything to eat? I let the guys take the rest of the soup home, but I could make you a salad or sandwich if you wanted."

"Thanks, but I've got some leftovers in the fridge that I should eat tonight," he told her. "I just wanted to say hi... and to ask if you're free tomorrow night."

"Sure, after the deli closes, of course. Did you have something in mind?" she asked. She was glad that the deli wasn't open very late; most evenings she could be home by eight and have a few hours before bedtime to finish whatever she hadn't been able to get done in the morning. If she did end up extending the deli's morning hours to include breakfast, she would have to rely more than ever on her employees. There was no way that she would be able to regularly work twelve-hour days without driving herself into the ground.

"Would you be interested in getting dinner with me at the Redwood Grill? I just closed another case, and I'd love to celebrate it with you," he said, his blue eyes twinkling as they met hers.

"I'd love to." A smile spread over her face. It sounded like work was going well for him too. It would be nice to spend an evening discussing their jobs; he might even have some good advice as to whether she should start serving breakfast or not.

"Great." He returned her smile with one of his own. "I'll pick you up at eight."

CHAPTER TWO

"I think you should do it," Candice said. Moira put the finishing touches on her hair before replying, making sure that no adventuresome strands would be able to escape during dinner.

"It will mean a lot of changes for both of us," she said at last. "And once you leave, I'll have to hire another employee. Maybe even two, considering how much you help out."

"But you want to expand eventually, don't you?" her daughter asked. "If breakfast ends up being a hit, then it could bring in the extra money you would need to open another place somewhere else. And if it doesn't work out, you can always just go back to the normal hours."

"You're right, as usual," Moira said with a laugh. "I'll run it by David tonight and see what he thinks."

"I'm sure he'll think it's a great idea. Have a good time, Mom." Candice gave her a quick hug as David's car pulled into the driveway. "Say hi to Denise for me."

Denise was the owner of the Redwood Grill, and she and Moira were now on friendly terms after a bumpy start to their relationship. She was glad; the two women had a lot in common. They were both business owners, they both worked with food, and they both had experience with lousy husbands. Her own ex had had an affair shortly before they divorced, and Denise was still trying to make a decision about whether or not she could trust her husband any longer. The two of them had begun getting together every Sunday evening to talk about the previous week over a glass or two of wine. Martha, another of Moira's friends, had also started joining them occasionally.

"I will if I see her," she promised her daughter. "I'll be back in a few hours." She grabbed her purse, bade her daughter a final goodbye, and opened the front door just as David reached the porch. She took his arm when he offered it, and the two of them made their way down the steps to his car.

"So, tell me about this case you just finished," she said as the waiter walked away. She sipped the glass of merlot, enjoying the smooth, rich flavor. The waiter had suggested it to go with the sizzling cut of steak she had ordered, and she had once again been impressed by how well the staff at the Redwood Grill knew their stuff.

"Oh, it was a corporate spy case," he said. "Nothing big, but I saved my client a few thousand dollars." He grinned. "Not quite as fun as some of the cases I've worked on with you. It was mostly a lot of background checking various employees, and following people around for hours every day."

"No wonder I haven't seen you much this week," she said. She worked odd hours on occasion, but it was nothing compared to the hours that David sometimes worked. She didn't know when he found time for sleep, not with the amount of time he spent driving around and tailing people. "And I wouldn't say my cases have been *fun* exactly... more like terrifying."

"Hmm... maybe fun wasn't the right word," he said.

"I think 'exhilarating' is the word I was looking for. None of my other cases have been as *exhilarating* as the ones you've gotten me involved with."

"That may be true," Moira replied with a laugh. "Still, I can't say I'm sorry that it's been quiet lately. Business is doing phenomenally well. I'm actually thinking of extending the hours that the deli is open for."

"Really?" he asked, leaning forward with obvious interest in his blue eyes. "That's great news. Are you thinking about doing breakfast hours?"

"Yes." She sighed. "But I'm not completely sure about it yet. I would need to come up with a whole new menu, find a few new suppliers, and would have to split about twenty extra hours a week between the four of us," she said, referencing herself, Dante, Darrin, and Candice. "It would mean more work, at least for a while."

"You would probably get quite a few new customers, though," he said. "Especially if you served coffee along with something easy to eat on the run, like muffins or quiches."

"Quiches?" Moira raised her eyebrows. "That's actually a great idea. I was thinking of doing some sort of breakfast sandwich, but I think quiches would be even better. I could put different ingredients in each day, and I could even do mini ones to make them even easier to eat on the run."

"Quiches it is, then," he said with a laugh. "It sounds like you've got it all planned out already." He paused to take a sip of his own wine before he asked, "How is Candice's search coming along?"

"Not well," she admitted. "She just hasn't been able to find a place as nice as that little toy shop, and Henry still hasn't gotten back to her."

"That's odd." David frowned, his brow wrinkling in consternation. Henry was an old friend of his—an avid fisherman prone to taking unexpected trips to his cabin up north. "It really isn't like him to be out of touch for so long."

"Do you think something might have happened to him?" she asked tentatively.

"Well, his granddaughter still insists that he's fine," he told her. "And it's not unusual for him to disappear for a while, it's just that he's always told me before." He shook his head, as if trying to clear bad thoughts from it. "I'm sure he's fine. He should be back soon, and when he is, I'll remind him to talk to Candice straight away."

"Thanks." Moira gave him a quick smile. "It would mean the world to her if she could buy, or even lease, the toy store and turn it into a candy shop. I hope she can be all set up before summer is over."

"Me too," he said. "I'll do what I can to help." They both looked up when the waiter appeared, pushing the dessert cart ahead of him. David traded a glance with her, and then ordered two lava cakes. *I'll need to buy a bigger belt if I keep this up*, Moira thought, but it was worth it. Not much could compare to good food and good company on a warm spring evening.

Once they had finished the scrumptious melted chocolate cakes, Moira excused herself, wanting to make a quick run to the restroom while David brought the car around. She kept her eyes peeled for Denise on her way back through the restaurant, finally spotting her friend chatting with an elderly couple seated at a small table. Not wanting to interrupt, she kept her distance until the redheaded woman had finished her conversation. Moira caught her eye and gave a small wave, and her friend glided over to her, weaving gracefully between tables and busy wait staff.

"It's wonderful to see you again, Moira. How was your food?" she said after giving the deli owner a quick hug.

"Amazing, as usual," Moira replied, grinning. "And as usual, I ate way too much."

"Nonsense," Denise said with a laugh. "You can't have too much of a good thing." A sly smile appeared on her face. "Are you here with David?"

"Yes." She tried to ignore the blush that she felt rising in her cheeks. "We got together to celebrate a case of his that he finished up the other day."

"I see." Her friend's eyes danced with amusement. "You two enjoy your evening. I've still got a few more hours before we close for the night, and then I have to go meet with my husband." Her lips pursed at this, as if even mentioning the man left a bad taste in her mouth.

"How are things with him?" Moira asked, lowering her voice so the conversation would stay between the two of them.

"Better, I suppose. At least we're on speaking terms." She sighed. "I think that this time apart has actually been good for us. With me so busy here, and him running the other restaurant by himself, we haven't really had time to argue."

"That's good. I hope you two figure things out. At least you have something that you're both passionate about," the deli owner said. "You both are phenomenal at running restaurants."

"Thanks." Her friend gave her a grateful smile. "I can't imagine how you run your little place all on your own."

"Oh, I have help. My employees are amazing, and my daughter has been helping a lot with the business aspects of it. I don't know what I'll do when she moves away," Moira said. "That's not to say that I'm not glad that she's following her dreams, of course, but I'll miss her."

"Of course you will. It's never easy when they leave home." Her friend gave her another quick hug. "I should be getting back to work. Have a nice evening, Moira."

"You too, Denise." She watched as her friend walked away, and then realized that she had left David waiting for longer than she should have. Feeling somewhat guilty for having been so distracted by Denise, she hurried through the restaurant and pulled the heavy doors open.

She was surprised to find herself walking into an argument. David and, of all people, Detective Fitzgerald, were standing face to face. She had never seen David look so angry before. No, actually she *had*, but only once, and that had been when he had saved her from the most recent madman who had tried to kill her. David was right; her life had been exhilarating lately.

Their conversation cut off when she stepped outside, and she hadn't been able to catch what they were saying. A few people were standing nearby, watching the argument with expressions ranging from amusement to fear. Both men looked over at her as she approached.

"David?" she said. "What's going on?"

"Nothing," he said, his voice oddly strained. He gave Fitzgerald one last glance, and then turned towards her. "Sorry, I didn't have a chance to get the car yet. Luckily we didn't park too far away."

Is he going to act like nothing weird just happened? Moira wondered, staring up at him for a long moment before glancing over towards the other man. The detective was standing still with his jaw clenched, glaring at *her*, for some reason. He didn't say anything, and Moira didn't want to address the issue with so many onlookers present.

"Let's go," she said to David, eager to get to the privacy of the car where she could ask him what on earth was going on. He followed her, his face still tense. It was strange to see the normally relaxed private investigator so worked up.

"What was that about?" she asked once she had slipped into the passenger seat and had shut the door firmly against the night.

"We were just having a discussion that got a little heated," he said shortly. "Sorry, I don't often lose my temper."

"What was the discussion *about?*" Moira asked, knowing that she shouldn't pry, but unable to hold back her curiosity.

"I'd rather not say," David said after glancing at her. She was surprised to see that he looked embarrassed, although she wasn't sure whether it was the fact that he had lost his temper or the mysterious subject of the argument. He paused at a stoplight and patted his pocket. "Darn it, I must have left my wallet there."

"We can go back and get it," she said. He thought about it for a moment, then shook his head. "No, we're almost back to your house. I'll drop you off, and then stop back on my way home." He still seemed a bit unsettled by his encounter with the detective, so Moira changed the subject.

"Thanks for taking me out to dinner," she said. "I had a really nice time, and I even got to see Denise right before I left. She's doing well; I'm really glad we've become friends."

David also seemed ready to forget about the argument and they talked about inconsequential topics until they reached her house. Moira realized that she felt more comfortable with David than she had

PATTI BENNING

with any of the other men she'd halfheartedly dated since her divorce and smiled at the private investigator as he walked her to her door.

"Thank you for another lovely evening, David. I really enjoy our... dates." She hesitated over the last word, not wanting to scare him off.

"No thanks necessary. I also enjoy myself thoroughly on our dates." He said the word more confidently than she had, and she smiled again. He continued, "we will do this again, yes?"

"Oh, yes." Moira was delighted and after a quick peck on his cheek, went inside. She had high hopes for this relationship, but she was happy he also wanted to take it slow.

CHAPTER THREE

Moira carefully stabbed a toothpick through the center of the last sandwich that she had made for Detective Fitzgerald's retirement party, then reached for the plastic wrap that would cover the platter. She and Candice had made over a hundred small sandwiches total, arranging them according to type on a few large plates. There was corned beef and swiss, honey-glazed ham with tomato and lettuce, and cold chicken breast with sharp cheddar cheese. She had also made a small plate of vegetarian sandwiches, knowing that at least a few of her regulars who were bound to be at the party would appreciate them.

She hadn't seen the detective since the unfortunate encounter at the Redwood Grill and she hoped that whatever had happened between him and David would have blown over by now. David still wouldn't tell her what the argument had been about. She had convinced him a few days ago to go with her and Candice to the detective's retirement party, but had spent the last few hours worrying about whether or not she had made the right decision in getting him to come. She hoped that whatever they had argued about hadn't been serious, and that the festive atmosphere would help to soothe any hard feelings.

"I found the dress, but I couldn't find the shoes you wanted," Candice said as she came in through the deli's front door. She was carrying a dark green dress draped over her arm and a pair of black shoes in her hand. "I hope these will do."

"Thanks, sweetie. They'll be fine."

Moira had been planning on wearing black slacks with a pale pink blouse to the party that evening, but the day had turned out to be unexpectedly nice— almost seventy degrees and sunny, to boot. It had been months since she had worn one of her nice summer dresses, and she so rarely had an occasion to really dress up that she decided not to waste her chance. Her daughter had been kind enough to run back to the house and pick the clothes up for her, since they were planning on going straight to the party from the deli after they closed.

"Did you get in touch with David?" her daughter asked.

"Yes, he said that he would meet us there. I guess he has something to do first; he'll probably be a few minutes late," Moira replied. "Which means we'll have to bring the sandwiches in on our own."

"I'm sure someone else will help us. Pretty much the entire police station will be there," the young woman pointed out.

"That's true," the deli owner said. "Oh, have you heard from Adrian? He's welcome to come too, you know."

"I think he's got something else going on." Candice's brow creased. "We haven't really been talking as much lately."

"I'm sorry, sweetheart." She had noticed that Candice and her boyfriend were growing apart over the last few weeks, but she had hoped that the two would remain friends. The young man definitely had a mind for business, and had been doing a lot to help Candice prepare for opening and running the candy shop.

"It's all right," her daughter replied. Her face brightened. "I'm young and single, and about to go to a party where half the town will probably turn up. Things could be worse."

They only spent another hour at the deli before Moira decided to call it a night and close a bit early. It was an unusually slow evening, and if someone was just dying for a sandwich they could always come to Detective Fitzgerald's retirement party and get a free one. She took a few minutes to change into the dark green dress in the deli's bathroom and fix up her hair, then she and her daughter loaded the sandwiches into the back of her car and left. The party was being held in the event space that took up most of the Town Hall's sizable basement, and it was only a few short minutes away from the deli.

Sure enough, a nice young officer met them at the door and offered to help bring in the platters of sandwiches. Moira balanced one of the large plates against her hip, and held the door for her daughter and the officer as they carried the others in. Relieved that they had managed to get all of the sandwiches inside in one trip—and without dropping any—she locked her car and followed the younger couple into the building and down the narrow stairway to the lower level of the building.

The Town Hall's basement was one of the most popular places for events in Maple Creek. It had held school dances, sweet-sixteens, even talent competitions. Moira had been there a few times over the years, and was always impressed by how nice the space was. There was a bar area, a dance floor, and a small room for simple food preparation. Tonight, the decorations were simple: a handmade banner reading *Thank You for Your Service* hung from the ceiling, and a pair of blue balloons were tied to each table. A few people were already milling around, chatting with each other or signing the guest book. Detective Jefferson greeted her just inside the door, stepping quickly to the side to hold it open for her as she trailed behind Candice.

"I'm glad you got here early; the sandwiches can just go on the table. Feel free to help yourself to the drinks or any of the snacks. The cake we're saving for later," he said.

"Thanks. Everything looks amazing." She looked around the room again, touched that so many people had turned up just to wish the older detective a happy retirement. "I wanted to say hi to Detective Fitzgerald, but I don't see him," she said after a moment. "Where is he?"

"He hasn't arrived yet." The young detective frowned. "He was supposed to be here half an hour ago. I hope everything is all right. I know that this is a tough milestone for him. He lives for his job."

"I know the feeling." Moira couldn't imagine retiring from working at the deli. What would she do with her days? Even in her spare time, she often did things for the deli, such as inventing new soup and sandwich combos, or visiting local farmers markets to find new suppliers for the fresh produce that she needed. Without the deli to focus on, she would likely have nothing better to do than sit around in her pajamas and catch up on all of her favorite shows. Which, she had to admit, did sound tempting on her busiest days.

"I'll point him in your direction when he shows up," Jefferson promised. "You can go ahead and drop those sandwiches off, and then enjoy the party."

The deli owner did as he suggested, pausing only to pour herself a cup of coffee before heading over to sign the guest book. She wrote, *Thank you for all you've done—Moira,* and then tapped the pen against her lower lip, not sure if she should add more. The older detective had helped to solve a couple of the cases that she had been dragged into, and she honestly didn't know where she would be right now if it wasn't for him. She decided to leave her note as it was; simple and to the point. He would surely recognize her name, and she could always thank him in person when he got here.

"Here you are. How's the party?" Moira turned around to find David standing a few feet behind her. He was holding his right arm gingerly, wincing slightly as he moved it to reach for the pen.

"The party would be better if the guest of honor were here, but it's still nice. Are you injured?" she said, unable to keep the concern out of her voice.

"Don't worry—it's nothing major. Since the weather is so nice, I took my bike out for the first time this year. Hit an unexpected patch of loose gravel, and fell on my shoulder." He shrugged, flinched, and then grinned ruefully. "It'll heal up fine, and it's a good reminder that I need to get back into shape."

"I'm glad it wasn't worse; Candice broke her arm riding a bike when she was younger." The deli owner laughed ruefully. "I don't even remember the last time I rode a bicycle. I think mine is gathering rust in the back of my garage."

"Maybe we can ride together when the weather is nicer." He scribbled his signature on the guest book, and then straightened up and looked around. "Did you just say that Fitzgerald isn't here?"

"Not unless he just arrived. Jefferson told me when I got here that he hasn't shown up yet," Moira said.

"Odd." David's forehead wrinkled into a frown for a second as he looked around.

"Oh, I almost forgot. Did you ever find your wallet?" she asked.

"No." He sighed. "Luckily it didn't have much cash in it, and I already canceled my cards." He shrugged, less bothered by the missing wallet than she would have been. "It's annoying, but I already got replacements. Where did you get that coffee? It smells delicious."

The party carried on, sans the guest of honor, for a good half hour before Moira saw detective Jefferson pull a young officer out of the crowd and drag him over to a secluded corner near her. She tried not to eavesdrop, but failed miserably. When she heard Jefferson tell the young man to go to Fitzgerald's house and see what was taking him so long, the first tendrils of real concern unfurled in her stomach. What if something bad had happened to the older man? She didn't know him well, but he didn't seem like the type to be late for his own party. Biting her lip, she stood up and looked around for David, hoping to ask him if he thought that there was any reason that she should be worried. She nearly bumped into a balding man about her age, who was watching the corner where Detective Jefferson was standing with an odd expression.

"Sorry, excuse me," she said quickly. He glanced over at her for a split second, during which she noticed pale gray eyes and an unusual tattoo peeking out from his collar.

"'S'alright," he mumbled, looking away from her again just as quickly. Trying to ignore the man's unpleasant smell of stale cigarette smoke and unwashed clothes, she looked around the room again, hoping to see David.

Instead of finding the tall, dark-haired private investigator, her gaze landed on another familiar face—that of her friend Martha Washburn. She had known the other woman for years, but their friendship had only really solidified recently, after Martha's sister's untimely death. Moira had been the one to find Emilia's body, which could have put a strain on their blossoming friendship if she hadn't also been the one who had saved Martha from meeting the same fate. The two women were closer than ever now, though they didn't get to see each other as much as either of them would have liked.

"I thought you might be here," Martha said, smiling as she reached out to hug her friend. "I was pretty sure that I recognized your sandwiches."

"Yep, Candice and I made them," Moira chuckled. "How are they? We worked all day, but still had to rush to get the last few made."

"Both of the ones I had were delicious," the other

woman assured her. "I'm positive that you've won yourself at least a few more loyal customers this evening."

Moira opened her mouth to thank her friend, but at that moment a commotion started near the entrance to the hall. A woman screamed and dropped to the floor, to be immediately surrounded by people eager to help. Detective Jefferson was on the phone, looking grim. A young officer was standing next to him, and Moira recognized him as the man that Jefferson had sent to check on Fitzgerald. He looked pale, and even from across the hall, she could see that he was shaking. David was approaching her quickly, and she hurried to meet him, leaving a confused Martha behind.

"What happened?" she asked, fear making her stomach clench.

"Something terrible." David took a deep breath. "Detective Fitzgerald is dead."

CHAPTER FOUR

"Wow, that's horrible." Darrin had paused in the middle of scrubbing the counter to listen while Moira told him about the detective's retirement party the night before. Now he was shaking his head, the rag forgotten. "Why would he do something like that?"

"I don't know, it just doesn't make sense," said Moira. "To serve over thirty years on the force, only to kill himself the night before his last day of work... it just seems so sad. I feel terrible for his wife."

"Are they sure that it was a suicide?" the young man asked.

"I only know what I overheard the young officer who found him tell Detective Jefferson. His name was Fier, I think. Officer Fier. He said that he found Fitzgerald surrounded by empty bottles of sleeping pills, with a bottle of whiskey in his hand." She sighed. "I hate to say it, but it really does sound like suicide. I'm sure they'll have more information in a few days, when the toxicology reports come in, though."

"I'm sorry you and Candice had to be there, but I'm almost glad that I decided to stay home and work on schoolwork instead of going." He sighed and picked up the rag again. "You just can't catch a break, can you, Ms. D?"

Leaving Darrin to finish tidying up before the deli opened, Moira slipped into the kitchen and began to get the ingredients out for the soup and sandwich combo of the day. She began by peeling a few cloves of garlic which she then slid into a pot along with some butter. She turned the heat to just below medium, and then pulled some chicken breasts out of the fridge where they had been defrosting. While the garlic sizzled, she trimmed the fat from the breasts and seasoned them lightly with salt and pepper. They would bake to perfection in the oven while she made the garlic soup, and would be served on toasted Italian bread with a thin spread of fresh pesto and just a squeeze of lemon juice, the perfect complement to the slightly sweet flavor of the roasted garlic in the soup. The combo would be light, yet intensely flavorful, and Moira was eager to see how her customers liked it.

The familiar routine of cooking distracted her from her thoughts of the detective's death, and helped her to feel better. No matter what else was going on in her life, she always had the deli to keep her focused and calm. It wasn't until the soup was simmering softly away, the chicken breasts were out of the oven and chilling in the fridge, and a fresh batch of pesto had been made that she took a break from cooking and decided to spend some time up front. She knew that, by now, nearly everyone in town would have heard of the detective's death, and of course would be wanting to talk about it. She would probably end up repeating her version of events more times than she could count, which she wasn't looking forward to. She couldn't avoid her customers forever, though, so, bracing herself, she decided to take over from

Darrin at the register and brave the gossip storm alone.

"Welcome to Darling's DELIcious Delights," she said, trying not to let her exhaustion show in her voice. "Our special today is garlic soup with a chicken and pesto sandwich."

"I'll take a sandwich, no soup. And could I get cheese on it?" the man asked. He looked like he was around thirty, with short spiky hair and a worn leather coat that had seen better days. She thought he looked slightly familiar. Had he been at the retirement party? Or maybe he had been one of the onlookers at the Redwood Grill during David's argument with Fitzgerald. She wasn't sure.

"Sure; what kind?" Moira asked. "We've got cheddar, swiss, Monterey-"

"Cheddar," he cut in. "Extra sharp."

Feeling a bit snubbed, but not letting it show, she poked her head into the kitchen and told Darrin the special order. Then she turned back to the man who was busy looking at, not the food, but the wall of photos and posters that she and her employees had put up a few weeks ago.

"Can I get you anything else?" she asked. "A drink, maybe?"

"I'm fine," he told her without turning around. A moment later, he looked over his shoulder and added, "Was it a fun party?" Moira looked up to see that he was staring at the flyer that gave the information for Fitzgerald's retirement party. Her stomach dropped. She really should have taken that down the second she got here this morning.

"No," she replied, walking out from behind the counter to yank the flyer off the wall. "The guest of honor passed away that evening."

"Oh, how sad." He looked at his watch and began tapping his foot impatiently. "What happened?"

"They think it was a suicide," she told him brusquely. It was with relief that she saw Darrin bringing out the man's food. "Your order's ready. Thanks for stopping in."

She was thankful that the next two customers didn't mention anything about Detective Fitzgerald or the retirement party. They both ordered a cup of soup to go along with their groceries, and left chatting happily together. It was another gorgeous day outside, if a bit chillier than yesterday. Normally such nice spring weather would have put the deli owner in a good mood, but today she just couldn't shake the bad feeling from the night before. Her temper brightened only slightly when she saw David's familiar black car pull into the parking lot.

"How are you doing?" he asked as he walked into the store.

"I've been better," Moira admitted. "I just can't stop thinking about what happened last night."

"Neither can I." He paused, examining the selection of cheeses in the display case. His face showed that he was having some sort of internal battle, as if deciding whether to tell her something. After a moment he sighed and walked over to the register. He glanced around to make sure that there was no one in the front room of the deli but them, and then said, "If I tell you something, can you promise not to get yourself involved in whatever is going on?"

"What's going on?" she asked, attempting to avoid promising anything that she might come to regret.

"Promise," he insisted.

"I can't promise anything until you tell me what it is." She gazed up at him, hoping that he would understand. He sighed and shook his head.

"Fine, but don't make me regret this." He took a deep breath. "Detective Fitzgerald didn't commit suicide. He was murdered."

"Oh, my goodness, how do you know?" She grabbed the counter as shock rushed through her. Someone had killed the detective on the day he was supposed to retire? Who could do such a thing?

"I stopped in at the Maple Creek police station to get a background check on someone for the case I'm working on," he told her. "And I overheard the younger detective, Jefferson, talking about it with an officer. He said that Fitzgerald didn't even have any pills in his stomach, but his body showed signs of suffocation. I'm guessing that they rushed the autopsy on him."

Moira shuddered, not wanting to think about the gory details. Then she began to think about what the news meant; someone had murdered the detective who had served the town for several decades. Once this became public news, there would be turmoil. No officer would rest until the murderer was found, and there would likely be a flood of false tips called in to the police station. She understood why David had hesitated to tell her; the police wouldn't be happy if this information got out before they were ready.

"I won't tell anyone," she promised. "I wouldn't want to do anything to mess up their investigation."

"That's good, but it's not what I asked," he said. "I don't want you involved, period."

"What do you think I'm going to do?" she asked, somewhat miffed. "It's not like I go *looking* for trouble. I don't like being chased by murderers, or stumbling across dead bodies."

"I know." David sighed and ran his hand through his hair. "It's just that trouble seems to have a way of finding you."

"Well, I don't see how I would get dragged into this case," she said. "It has nothing to do with me, or the deli, or any of my employees."

"Good," he said. "I hope it stays that way."

He still looked worried, so Moira decided to change the subject. She understood that he didn't want her to be in danger, but it hurt that he thought that she would go looking for trouble. She had been cherishing the peace of the last couple of months, and besides, she would do anything to keep herself and her daughter away from whoever had killed Detective Fitzgerald.

"Do you want a bowl of soup and a sandwich?" she asked him. She gestured to the blackboard where the day's special was written. "It's a new combo, and it's been quite the hit so far."

"Sure." He gave her a tired smile. "If you join me, we can talk about one of my new cases."

"It's a deal." She flashed him a grin, then pushed through the door to the kitchen to get their food.

"So, tell me about this case," she said, taking a bite of her sandwich. The strong flavors of basil, Romano cheese, and pine nuts burst in her mouth. The cold sandwich was a wonderful pairing with the warm garlicky soup. This was definitely one of her new favorite combos.

"Well, a few days ago, I was contacted by an elderly lady in Lake Marion who said her beloved dog had been stolen. Of course, at first I thought it must have just run away, but I agreed to take the case anyway since it was obvious that she was distraught." He paused for a spoonful of soup. "However, when she showed me her house and her yard, I realized that it was very unlikely that the dog ran away. The gate to her backyard is on a spring, so it closes automatically—couldn't have been left open—and she only ever uses the back door to go in and out. All of her windows have screens on them, so the dog couldn't have gotten out that way. It was a real mystery."

"Did you solve it?" Moira asked, fascinated by the story. His life must be so much more interesting than hers, but more dangerous, too. "Did you find the dog?"

"Not yet," he said with a grimace. "But the really interesting part comes a few days later, when a few other people came in complaining of stolen dogs. The total is up to five now, and I'm sure there are more that haven't reported it yet."

"So, someone is out there stealing people's pets? That's terrible." She hadn't had a pet in a couple of years, but the dog that they had had while Candice was growing up had been a part of the family. It had been hard to let the fourteen-year-old Labrador go, and Moira and her daughter had both been too heartbroken to get another pet right away.

"I've been doing everything I can to find them, but haven't had a lead so far," he told her.

"I hope that nothing bad happens to those dogs," she said. "People that hurt animals are especially terrible."

"You *can* help me out on this if you want," he said. He reached into his pocket and pulled out a folded piece of paper. "This has a picture of each missing dog on it. If you see someone walking one of these dogs, or driving with it in a car, you should call me right away."

"I'll keep my eyes peeled," she promised, taking the paper from him and unfolding it. Most of the missing dogs were purebreds. There was a picture of an apricot poodle, a chubby beagle, a gorgeous collie, a blue-eyed husky, and a little black mixed breed with long fur.

"Remember, *call* me. Don't get involved." He looked like he was already regretting giving her the paper, so she folded it up and slid it into her pocket.

"I'll call," she assured him. "Don't worry, I want to stay as far away from criminals as possible.

CHAPTER FIVE

The following day was one of Moira's rare days off. Dante and Darrin were at the deli, and though she would be available if they needed her, both of them had assured her that they would be able to manage fine without her. It was never easy leaving the deli in someone else's hands, but she trusted the young men, and knew that going too long without a day off wasn't good for her.

She had a few things that she wanted to do during her free day; ironically, number one on her mental list was to figure out just how much more work would be required if they started opening the deli in time for breakfast. After waking up unusually early and grabbing a cup of steaming, rich Columbian coffee, she sat down at the dining room table with a pad of paper and her account book, and began looking at the numbers. She would definitely have to hire a new employee soon in any case, with Candice about to leave to start her own business. If she were to extend the deli's hours, she would likely need to take on two new employees, which, along with the extra hours, would add up to quite a bit more that she would be paying in wages each month.

The question was, would they end up bringing in enough extra money through the sale of breakfast items to make up the difference? It was a hard question to answer, but after she did some math and played around with the existing schedules for a bit, she thought the answer might be yes. As long as they got at least as many people in for breakfast as they did for lunch most days, then the deli would end up making a profit, even after the additional expenses.

That wasn't taking into account the extra hours of electricity, of course, or the cost of new packaging materials or appliances, but she was pretty sure that they would be able to make it work. She leaned back in her chair, impressed by what she had accomplished already that morning. All that was left was to find a couple of new suppliers, figure out if she was willing to commit the extra hours of her own time, and see if Dante was actually any good at making quiches.

"I thought I smelled coffee," said Candice as she walked down the stairs. She paused to yawn and stretch, still in her pajamas. "Isn't this your day off, Mom? Why do you look like you're working?"

"Just figuring out some stuff for the deli." Moira gulped down the last dregs of her now lukewarm coffee. "What are your plans for the day?" She knew that Candice wasn't scheduled at the deli for the next two days, but hadn't yet asked her daughter why she had requested the time off.

"I'm going over to Samantha's house," the young woman said. "We're going shopping, and then I'm going to spend the night at her place. We're planning on having a movie night."

"Oh. That sounds nice." She couldn't help but feel somewhat disappointed that her daughter wouldn't be around for the day. *I'd better get used to being alone in this house,* she thought. *Soon enough, she's going to live in another town.* "Have a good time, sweetie."

"I'm sure we will; she just got one of those new smart TVs that can play things in 3D." Candice yawned again. "Any coffee left?"

A few hours later, after her daughter had gotten dressed and left, Moira found herself kneeling on the bathroom floor scrubbing at the tiles with a rag. She was rarely so bored as to have to entertain herself with cleaning, but today was one of those days where she wasn't in the mood to watch television, she didn't have anything good to read, and there were no pressing errands. She could always go into the deli and see if the boys needed any help, but she didn't want to give up on having a day off quite yet. Surely she'd find the secret to relaxing soon.

It wasn't until she began a load of laundry that she found the folded-up paper with the pictures of the missing dogs in her pocket. She gazed at the somewhat blurry photos of the pooches for a few moments, an idea slowly forming in her mind. It was just after noon, so she had the whole afternoon in front of her. Instead of puttering around the house, why not go into town and do some window shopping, while keeping an eye out for the missing pets? She had promised David that she wouldn't go looking for trouble and she would be mostly keeping her promise. After all, a day spent out in town could hardly be considered looking for trouble, and if she just *happened* to see one of the missing dogs, she might be able to help the private investigator with his case and reunite the beloved pets with their frantic owners.

Her mind made up, and feeling much better knowing that she had something to keep her occupied for a few hours at least, Moira finished putting the load of laundry into the washer, then headed upstairs to get ready to go out. The house still felt oddly quiet without Candice there, so to combat the silence, she turned the radio on for company as she did her hair and makeup. She had never liked living alone, and the thought that Candice would be moving out for good in just a few short months made her melancholy.

Maybe I should adopt a dog, she thought, her mind still on the missing pets that David was trying to find. *It would be nice to have someone to take care of once Candice moves out, and I would be able to give an animal in need a loving home.* Then again, if she did decide to expand the deli's hours, she might not have time for a pet. She heaved a sigh and leaned towards the mirror to fix a smudge in her eyeliner. She was always either working too hard or nearly going out of her mind with boredom. She really had to find a middle ground, and fast, or she would lose her mind.

She parked her car at the deli, partially out of habit, and partially because it wouldn't make sense to pay for a spot along the street when she could use her own business's parking lot for free. Resisting the urge to poke her head in the store and see how things were going, she locked the car, swung her purse over her shoulder, and made her way down the sidewalk towards the rest of the shops that lined Main Street.

Window shopping quickly became real shopping when she saw a cute blouse in the window of Another Man's Treasure, the secondhand shop that was run by an elderly couple. She stopped in and greeted Mrs. Zimmermann, then spent the next few minutes browsing. She spent the better part of an hour like that, weaving in and out of the small businesses on Main Street and greeting the owners by name when she knew them, and learning them when she didn't. Most people were familiar faces: they were her regulars, the people that came into the deli every week to pick up their special order of cheese, or to grab the deli's daily combo for lunch.

When clouds began to rush in, obscuring the sun and lending a sharp chill the air, she decided that it was time to head back to her car. She had kept her eyes peeled for any sign of the missing dogs, but hadn't seen any that even somewhat resembled the pictures that David had given her. *Of course, the thief probably isn't going to be stupid enough to prance around town in the middle of the day with stolen animals,* she thought. David had probably only asked her to help out with this case to keep her away from the mystery surrounding Detective Fitzgerald's death. *Why does he want me to stay away from that case so badly?* she wondered.

She rounded the corner, and was surprised to see David's car parked next to hers in the deli's parking lot. What was he doing here? Maybe he had news on the missing dogs. After pausing by her car to drop off her purchases, she let herself into the deli to find the private investigator leaning against the counter near the register and chatting with Darrin.

"Hey, Ms. D," her employee said, looking up as she came in. "How's your day off going?"

"Well, I got some shopping done," she said. "But it looks like I still ended up coming in."

"I saw your car," David said. "I stopped in to say hi, but Darrin told me that you weren't working today."

"I only came in because I saw that you were here, David. I wasn't planning on stopping in, I promise," she told Darrin with a laugh. "I'm perfectly capable of going a day without working." *Unless you count the finances and planning I did this morning,* she thought guiltily. *But I'll just keep that to myself.*

David started to reply, but fell silent, his eyes looking over Moira's shoulder, past her and towards the window that overlooked the parking lot. She turned, following his gaze, and saw Detective Jefferson getting out of his squad car, his two-way radio in hand and a frown on his face. She wondered what he was doing here. By his expression, he wasn't after a midday snack.

"Ms. Darling," he said as he walked in, inclining his head towards her in greeting, and then fixing his gaze on David. "Mr. Morris. I'm going to need to ask you to come with me, please."

"Why?" the private investigator asked. He looked confused. "Is this about one of my cases?"

"No. I just need to ask you some questions down at the station." He frowned. "Do you want to follow me there, or would you rather I give you a ride?"

"I'll follow." David shared a quick, befuddled look with Moira. "I'll call you later," he promised.

What was going on? she wondered. Had he made a mistake while investigating something for a client? Or perhaps the police had found the person responsible for the rash of pet thieveries. But no, the detective had told him that this wasn't about one of his cases.

Confused and concerned, she watched as David got in his car. As he pulled out of the parking lot right behind the police detective's vehicle, she turned to Darrin, who looked just as confused as she did.

"I've got no idea what that was about," he told her. "But whatever it is, I doubt it's serious. It's David, after all. He wouldn't commit a crime, would he?"

CHAPTER SIX

The next morning, Moira woke up early so she could meet David. He'd called after leaving the police station, but said they needed to speak in person, not over the phone. She had agreed to see him before she went into the deli, then spent a sleepless night wondering what on earth the police could have wanted with him.

Before he'd called, she had been unable to focus on the book that she'd picked up in town the day before, so she resorted to the one activity that always relaxed her: cooking. The results were stored in glass Tupperware containers in the fridge. Creamy chicken and dumpling stew, fried green beans, and homemade cheesecake-flavored pudding. She pressed a sticky note on the fridge, then set out a bowl and a soup spoon for Candice when she got home. She hoped that her daughter would see the note about the leftovers when she got home and would eat them instead of making something else.

She and David were meeting at a local animal shelter. The drive only took her about twenty minutes, but she had a hard time remaining patient even for that short time. She was relieved to see that his car was already in the parking lot when she got there, and she hurried to unbuckle her seatbelt, grab her purse, and go in. He met her at the front door.

"I'm glad you could make it," he said, giving her a quick smile as he held the door for her. "I know you've got work later, but this shouldn't take long."

"What are we doing here?" she asked, looking around. They were the only people in the reception room, other than the receptionist reading a magazine behind the front desk. The air held a strange mixture of the scents of cleaning solution and dog. There was a cacophony of barking from the back.

"I thought I might as well check the shelter again to see if any of the dogs have shown up. It's a good place to have a private discussion, too. No one will overhear us with that racket." He inclined his head towards the room with the barking dogs.

"I've been thinking a little about getting a dog again," she admitted as they walked back. "I just don't know if I would have time for it."

"Couldn't you bring one to work with you?" he asked. "It's not like you'd have to ask permission from the boss."

"I couldn't," she said reluctantly. She loved the idea, but couldn't risk it. "Not with all of the food there. Plus, some of my customers are bound to be allergic to dogs." She paused as they stepped through the door to the indoor kennel, where dogs of all shapes and sizes were kept. The noise of the barking swelled for the moment when the dogs heard the door open, and then declined again to more manageable levels. A quick look down the aisles showed that they were the only humans in the room.

"So, are you finally going to tell me what happened yesterday at the police station?" she asked as David began walking slowly down the first aisle, peering closely at each dog to see if it was one of the missing ones. "I've been worried out of my mind."

"Long story short," he said, "they think I might have killed Detective Fitzgerald."

Aghast, Moira stopped walking. She couldn't imagine the normally calm detective even getting into a fistfight, let alone committing murder. To make matters even more confusing, Detective Jefferson knew David pretty well; the private investigator often shared info with the police department about cases that he was working on. How could he seriously consider David to be a murder suspect?

"Why would they think that?" she asked.

"Well…" he hesitated. "They have some pretty good evidence tying me to Fitzgerald's place the night of his death."

"What did they find?" she asked, confused. As far as she knew, David hadn't been anywhere near Fitzgerald's house that night. They had been at his retirement party, for goodness sake. Plenty of people must have seen him there.

"My wallet," he told her. "They found my wallet there."

Shocked, Moira looked up into his face. He looked worried, but not terrified. The fact that he wasn't in jail was a good sign, she supposed. She knew from experience just how terrible it felt to be a person of interest in a murder investigation, and for his sake, she hoped that whatever was going on got cleared up quickly.

"But you lost your wallet the night we went out. That was a few nights before the party." she said, struck by sudden realization. He nodded. "Did you tell the police that?"

"Yeah," he said. He turned back to the row of kennels, resuming his slow walk down the aisle. "I could tell that they didn't believe me, though. *I* wouldn't have believed me. It sounds like a convenient lie." He shook his head. "To make matters worse, they've had a couple of witnesses come forward to say that they saw me arguing with the detective that night at the Redwood Grill."

"That doesn't mean anything, though. I mean, plenty of people argue. The two of you didn't come to blows or anything." She bit her lip, unable to shake the heavy weight of worry on her chest. *She* knew that

David hadn't killed anybody, but the police probably weren't going to be quite as easy to convince.

"It's still the only lead they've got, Moira," he said softly. "And what I said before is even more important now. Stay away from this case; I don't want you to get drawn into this."

She heard real concern in his voice, and understood that he was serious. The police would be turning over every rock as they tried to solve this crime; one of their own had been killed, after all.

"I don't see how they could tie you to the crime," she said, trying to be reassuring. "Obviously I didn't have anything to do with it. Not that you did, either," she added quickly. "But they don't have any evidence tying me to the crime. How did your wallet get there, anyway?"

"It was either planted, or Fitzgerald found it after our argument. I must have dropped it outside the restaurant." He rubbed his forehead. "I just don't understand why he wouldn't have returned the wallet to me if he had been the one to find it."

"I'm sure he would have returned it the second he found it," she said, remembering how serious the detective had always been about his job. She couldn't imagine him keeping David's wallet just to spite him for some petty argument. "So, it must have been planted." She frowned as she realized just what that meant. Someone who hadn't hesitated to kill the cop was for some reason also targeting David. No wonder the private investigator wanted her to stay away from the case. They were dealing with a very dangerous person.

"I think so, too." He paused, bending down to get a closer look at a poodle, then rose with a sigh. "Wrong gender," he said.

"None of the missing dogs have up yet?" she asked. She knew that the longer a person was missing, the lower the chances of them being found alive. The same must hold true for pets.

"Nope. And even more have disappeared. I'm really at a loss with this case."

"I'm sorry. I wish I could help." She looked around at the pooches, each one waiting for the right person to come in and take them home. "I hope all of them are found safe, and get reunited with their owners." *And I hope that they catch Fitzgerald's real killer quickly,* she thought. *David doesn't deserve this. No one should have to worry about being arrested for a crime that they didn't commit, least of all someone like him who has done so much good for the community.*

CHAPTER SEVEN

She got to the deli with just enough time to spare
before opening to get a head start on the day's
special. Soon, the rich scent of mushrooms sizzling
in butter filled the kitchen. She tossed some cubed
beef into another pot, and her stomach rumbled as
the meat began to brown. The beef and mushroom
soup was an old recipe and a popular favorite. She
couldn't wait to have some for lunch, but first came
the familiar routine of opening the deli for business.
Dante arrived just as she was switching on the lights
in the display cases, and he gave her a quick wave as
he let himself in through the front door.

"It smells great in here already," he said. "I bet we'll
be busy today. Who wouldn't want a cup of hot soup

on such a gray day?" The weather was overcast and chilly, with a misty drizzle that made everything feel damp. It was indeed the perfect day for a warm cup of soup, though first her customers would have to brave the unpleasant weather to make it to her store.

"Feel free to grab a bowl for lunch," she told him. "It'll be ready in about ten minutes. I'm glad you got here early; there's actually something that I want to try." She led him back into the kitchen and, after pausing to give the soup a quick stir, took a carton of eggs out of the refrigerator.

"I've been thinking more about opening the deli for breakfast," she explained. "And I went over the numbers yesterday. I think it's a good idea, but there's still a few things that we need to figure out." She grinned at him. "You said you could make quiches, right? So, let's put them to the test. There's a mini muffin pan in the cupboard, and a whole batch of fresh eggs. All of the other ingredients that you'll need should be in the fridge or pantry."

"Are we going to sell these?" he asked, giving the eggs a nervous look. "I've really only ever cooked for my foster family and friends before."

"We'll set them up in one of the display cases out

front as free samples today," she assured him. "Just relax and do what you normally do. If people like them, we can start selling them once we extend the hours. I'm also going to buy a juicer and a new coffee maker, so people will have a few beverages to choose from."

"All right. I'll do my best," he promised.

"That's all I want." She gave him a quick, reassuring smile, then left him to it.

"Hello, and welcome to Darling's DELIcious Delights," she said, looking up from the register as the front door swung open. It had been a busy afternoon, but they were finally slowing down a little bit before the dinner rush. "Our daily special is written on the blackboard. Let me know if I can help you with anything."

The woman smiled at her, and then began to browse the selection of cold cuts. Moira's gaze drifted past her to the view outside. The weather was still drab, but at least the rain had stopped. Someone was walking down the sidewalk with a couple of dogs— an apricot colored poodle, and a chubby beagle. The difference in build between the two dogs made her smile, but the expression quickly faded as she realized what she was looking at. A poodle and a beagle; the same breeds as two of the missing dogs. Thinking quickly, she pulled her cell phone out of her pocket and snapped pictures until the trio had disappeared from view. Whoever it was had their hood up, but there might be something about the person that David or the police would recognize. Then she hit speed dial and put the phone to her ear. Hopefully David was still in town, because she may have just solved his case.

CHAPTER EIGHT

"No sign of him?" Moira asked, disappointed to see David walking back into the deli empty-handed.

"No." He sighed. "He's probably long gone. Can I see those pictures again?"

"Sure." She handed him her phone. "I'm sorry. I should have done more. I could have followed him, at least."

"I'm glad you didn't. I don't like the thought of you putting yourself in danger." He handed her back her phone after scrolling through the pictures of the hooded person and the dogs for a second time. "It's definitely two of the dogs. Can you send me a couple of the clearer ones? I may get lucky and see someone wearing the same outfit in town, and I want to be able to compare things quickly. I wouldn't want to nab the wrong guy."

"Of course, hang on." She swiped through her phone's gallery, selecting a few of the better images and attaching them to an email, which she then sent to David. "At least you know two of the dogs are still alive," she said.

"Yes, that's good news. I don't want to tell the owners just yet, though. I wouldn't want to give them false hope." He fell silent as someone came through the deli's front door, stepping back so that Moira could help the customer. The man grabbed a raspberry-flavored sparkling water from the refrigerator, and ordered a bowl of the beef and mushroom soup at the register.

Moira's eyes kept flicking between the man and her fingers as she punched his purchases into the register. He looked familiar, but she wasn't able to place him until he turned his head to look at the cheese wheel in the display case and she saw the tattoo on his neck. He had been at Detective Fitzgerald's retirement party; she remembered him because he had been watching Detective Jefferson so closely. He looked better now than he had then—less tired, and healthier. She handed him his receipt and the paper bag with his to-go bowl of soup in it without saying a word, and watched him leave.

"I've seen that guy before," she explained to David in a hushed voice. She told him about seeing him at the retirement party, and how she recognized him today from his tattoo.

"He was watching Detective Jefferson while he was getting the news about Fitzgerald," she continued. "Do you think he had something to do with Fitzgerald's death?"

"It could be." He glanced at the receipt in her hand. "He paid with his credit card, didn't he? Give me his name, and I'll see if I can pull up any information on him when I get back to the office."

"His name is Shawn Dietz," she told him. "Let me know if you find anything."

"I will," he promised. "Thanks for calling me about the guy with the dogs. You've given me hope that this case may have a happy ending yet."

Shortly after David left, Dante emerged from the kitchen. "The quiches are done," he said. "Do you want to try one?"

"Definitely. Why don't you bring a platter out? We can start offering them to customers and see how people like them," she suggested.

"All right, hang on." The young man went back into the kitchen, reappearing a few minutes later carrying a large platter of mini-quiches.

"Those look great," the deli owner said. She grabbed one and bit into it, enjoying the strong cheesy flavor. "And they taste amazing," she added.

"I hope customers think so, too," he said nervously.

"I'm sure they will," she reassured him. "They taste delicious, and they are the perfect size for people to grab on their way to work or school. Paired with a glass of freshly squeezed juice, or a cup of coffee, and breakfast should be a hit." She knelt down to rearrange some of the meats in the display case to make room for the quiches, then slid the tray onto the shelf and covered it with a glass lid.

"We should probably start advertising that we're extending our hours," she said after a moment's thought. "Could you make a poster or a flyer for us to hang in the window? I figure we can start with the new hours in two weeks, which should give us enough time to find another employee and rearrange when everyone works. We'll try opening at seven, and see how that works."

"I'll get started right away," he said. "I'm glad you liked the quiche." He disappeared back into the kitchen. Moira grabbed a sticky note, wrote *Free Samples* on it, and stuck it on the platter with the quiches. She looked around the little deli, feeling proud. It had been over two years since she had opened it, and she had come so far in such a short span of time. Her one-woman operation was now a popular shop with three employees besides herself. If the extended hours went as well as she hoped, then she would have extra money that she could use to expand even further, and maybe start serving more warm food or even possibly open a second store in a nearby town.

There were only two things currently dampening her spirits. The first was Detective Fitzgerald's untimely death and the fact that David was a suspect in the murder. And the second was the thought of those poor missing dogs and their frantic owners. She hoped that both cases would be resolved quickly, and despite the private investigator's insistence that she not get involved, she planned on helping in any way that she could.

The quiches turned out to be quite a success, with the platter completely emptied long before they closed the deli for the evening. She was glad that the little bite-sized snack had been popular, both because it meant that she would have something to feed her customers when they began stopping by for breakfast, and because it gave Dante a much-needed confidence boost. It looked like her expansion plans would work out well.

CHAPTER NINE

After saying goodbye to her employee, Moira sat in her car in the parking lot for a moment, going over the grocery list on her cell phone. There was nothing on it that she needed for the shop, but they were definitely running low on some of the basics at the house. She sighed, setting the phone down on the passenger seat and starting the engine. She might as well buy groceries now; she wouldn't be any more eager to go shopping in the morning.

As she was walking down the aisles at the grocery store, she kept her eyes peeled—as always—for ingredients that might make for tasty new soup or sandwich recipes. To her surprise, she found a familiar face instead of new ingredients; Detective

Jefferson had just turned down the same aisle that she was in. He waved to her, and she nodded back as they passed. She paused, biting her lip and trying to make up her mind, then turned her cart around and followed him. He raised his eyebrows as she approached, but paused to wait for her.

"Sorry," she said. "I won't keep you long. It's just... you don't really think that David did it, do you?"

"I thought you might ask something like that," he said with a sigh. He glanced over his shoulder to make sure they were alone in the aisle. "Between you and me," he said quietly, "I don't."

"Then why did you have to bring him in? He's done so much for the people in both Maple Creek and Lake Marion," she said. "And I know from experience what it feels like to be wrongly accused of something. It doesn't feel good."

"I may not think he did it," the detective said. "But I still have to do my job. A good investigator wouldn't ignore evidence that's right in front of his face just because it points to a guy that they think is innocent. That's not how the police work." He paused. "It's not what Detective Fitzgerald would have wanted."

"You're right." She frowned. "I'm sorry. I know you're just doing your job. I just wish that David didn't have to be the one to suffer for it."

"I agree that this whole situation is unfair. Listen, Ms. Darling, the evidence pointing to him is pretty heavy. We found his wallet at the crime scene, the two had just had a pretty bad argument, and David showed up late to the retirement party, favoring an arm." He met her gaze. "Like I said, I don't think that it was him, but until the evidence says otherwise, I'm going to have to keep viewing him as a suspect."

"Well, would it help if I told you that he noticed the missing wallet driving home after we had dinner at the Redwood Grill?"

The detective looked at her sternly. "*Did* he, or are you just saying he did?"

"Of course he did," she said with some heat. "I wouldn't lie about something like that."

Detective Jefferson sighed and rubbed his face. "I'm sorry. I know you wouldn't. It's been a hard week."

"I hope you catch the guy who really did it," she told him. "And I'm sorry about Fitzgerald. I didn't know him that well, but from what I could tell, he was good at his job and really cared about the town."

"He did," the detective said. "And thanks. I'll miss him. He was a good man."

By the time she got home, all she wanted to do was to put the groceries away and go to bed. It had been a long day, and a lot had happened. When Candice greeted her at the door, she started to tell her daughter about everything that had happened, but the young woman interrupted.

"Mom, you've got to see this," she said, grabbing Moira's arm and half leading, half dragging her to the living room where their old desktop computer was set up.

"What is it?" the deli owner asked, truly exhausted and not prepared to deal with anything else.

"Just read," her daughter said impatiently.

Moira sighed and sat in the seat, squinting at what was on the screen. It was an article from the Maple Creek news website. The headline read *Private Investigator Questioned About Detective's Murder.* She was surprised to see a shot of David under the headline.

The picture showed him walking from his office in Lake Marion to his car, and it was obvious that he wasn't aware of the photographer. She perused the rest of the article quickly. It said pretty much what she expected; that David had been brought in for questioning about Detective Fitzgerald's murder, and that he had been seen arguing with the detective in a public area a few days beforehand. There wasn't any mention either of the wallet or David's late arrival to the party, which was a relief. Whoever the source was for the article, they didn't seem to know as much about this case as they had when they were reporting about Moira's supposed involvement with Henry Devou's death a few months ago.

"I'm really starting to dislike our local news," she said, turning off the computer screen and rising out of the chair.

"I know you like him, Mom." Candice hesitated, not meeting her mother's gaze. "But... do you think that he could have done it?"

"Of course not," Moira said quickly. "He would never do something like that."

"You haven't even known him for that long," her daughter pointed out. "For all you know, he could be like a serial killer or something." The young woman saw the look on her mother's face and backpedaled quickly. "Okay, so he probably isn't. But you have to admit, there is a possibility that he isn't who you think he is."

Is Candice right? Moira wondered. They really hadn't known David for more than a few months. The private investigator had never been anything but kind and helpful to her, but she knew from experience that even a cold-hearted killer could be polite. And the truth was, there was even more evidence pointing towards David than her daughter knew. His wallet *had* been found in Fitzgerald's house, and although there was a good explanation for that, she clearly remembered him showing up late and injured to the detective's retirement party. He had said that he'd had a biking accident, and she hadn't questioned it, but now she couldn't help but wonder. What if his injuries had actually been from attacking and murdering the older detective?

She shook her head to clear it. What was she thinking? This was David; she might not have known him for long, but she *did* know him well, and he would never kill anyone. She must be more tired than she thought if she was actually considering him as a suspect.

"I just don't think that he could have done it," she told Candice. Covering up a yawn with one hand, she asked, "Could you help me bring in the groceries? I'm exhausted. We can talk more tomorrow."

CHAPTER TEN

For the next few days, life went as usual in the quiet town of Maple Creek. The warm spring weather and sunny days returned, and business at the deli was booming. Moira was glad that the icy days of winter were past; spring wasn't her favorite season—she preferred summer—but it was a close second. There was something wonderful about walking through the park with warm, fresh-smelling air, and watching the first green buds beginning to appear on the trees. Soon enough, it would be swimming season, and she and Candice could travel the half hour to Lake Michigan on weekends. She loved spending the day at the beach, even if the water was usually chilly well into summer. If they had time, they might even be able to take a trip to the warmer shores on the other side of the state. Lake Huron was a favorite vacation spot for their family, and it was always nice to travel.

It was a slow Wednesday afternoon at the deli when Candice came in with excitement all over her face. Moira looked up from her novel and immediately knew that her daughter must have good news of one kind or another.

"What happened, sweetheart?" she asked.

"I found an apartment," her daughter exclaimed. "It's perfect, and right in town. It overlooks Main Street in Lake Marion. Will you come see it with me when I go to put the security deposit down?"

"Of course." Moira smiled at the beaming young woman, feeling guilty for her suddenly complex feelings. This was it; her daughter was really going to move out, and soon. "When were you going to go?"

"Right now. Can you come?"

"I don't know... it's right in the middle of the day..."

"Mom, you're sitting at the register reading a book. I saw both Darrin and Dante's cars out there; couldn't one of them watch the store for just, like, an hour?" Her daughter's eager expression made Moira laugh.

"Okay, okay, I'll let them know I'm leaving," she said. "Hold on just a second."

She followed her daughter into Lake Marion, taking the time to admire the forest that lined the curving, winding road. The scenery really was beautiful, with ferns and other small plants just beginning to peek through the ground. Almost all of the snow was gone by now, though she spotted a few stubborn piles hidden in areas where direct sunlight rarely, if ever, reached.

Her daughter parked behind the building that housed the small toy store that would, with any luck, one day become Candice's candy shop. Moira locked her car, and then followed the young woman over to a door set into the side of the building.

"It's up here," her daughter said. "That way, if I do end up being able to lease the toy store, or buy it if they decide to sell, I'll be right above my shop. Even if I end up renting a different space for the candy store, I'll still be living in a nice, central area."

"I'm eager to see it," Moira said. "Your first place. It's so exciting." She shared a smile with her daughter, then followed the young woman up the narrow staircase. There were only two doors at the top, and her daughter opened the one on the right.

Moira had been expecting a small, cramped area, so she was surprised when she walked into a room that had high ceilings, gorgeous hardwood floors, and shiny new appliances. Even though it was a small apartment, the spacious ceilings and generous windows made it feel much larger than it was. The kitchen had granite counter tops and a huge sink, with a stainless steel fridge that put even the deli's refrigerator to shame.

The dining room and living room were an open plan, and the living room area opened out onto a small balcony overlooking Main Street. The single bedroom was small, but not tiny, about the size of Candice's bedroom at Moira's house. She was envious of the shower in the bathroom; it was large, with a bench seat and a beautiful slate floor.

"Wow, this place is amazing," she told her daughter. "How did you find it?"

"Adrian heard about it from a friend and told me," she said.

Are you two back together?" Moira knew that Candice was lucky in a lot of ways, but not when it came to men. She didn't know much about the breakup with Adrian, only that he hadn't been coming around the deli as much over the past few weeks.

"No, but we're still friends. He's still planning on helping me with the candy shop," her daughter said. "Isn't this place just perfect, though? And it's a pretty good price, too. What do you think, should I put the deposit down?"

"If you like this apartment, then go for it," the deli owner said. "Just be completely sure that you want to open your business in Lake Marion. It wouldn't be good if you had already put the deposit down on this place, and then decide you want to open the candy shop in Traverse City."

"I'm sure," the young woman replied. "This is the perfect town for my candy shop. Besides, Traverse City is too far from you and the deli. I would never move there." Moira hugged her daughter; it was good to know that Candice felt the same way about moving out.

Since she was already in town, after leaving Candice with the real estate agent at her soon-to-be new apartment, Moira decided to call David and see if he was free to get a cup of coffee. He answered almost immediately when she called, and they agreed to meet up at the small coffee shop on the corner of Main and Pine Streets.

Moira got there first and ordered a caramel cappuccino, then seated herself at a small table in the back. She realized that the first time she had ever met David had been at a coffee shop. It seemed like so long ago, but in reality had been far less than a year.

"So, Candice found an apartment?" David asked as he slid into the seat across from her, a mocha in hand.

"She did, and I'm surprised by how nice it is." She spent a few minutes describing the little apartment to him. The thought of Candice living in the same town as the private investigator comforted her. She knew that if Candice ever needed help, she would be able to call David.

"I'm going to miss her," she finished. "But I'm glad that she's beginning to live her own life. I really hope that this candy shop venture works out for her."

"If she's got anything like your mind for business, I'm sure it will." He smiled at her, and Moira noticed for the first time how tired he looked.

"Are you all right?" she asked. "You look exhausted."

"I haven't been sleeping well lately," he said. "This whole murder investigation thing has really been getting to me."

"Oh." She hadn't told him about the news article that she had read online, but he had likely found it by now anyhow. "Have they brought you in for questioning again?"

"Not yet," he said. "But business hasn't been going so well. No one wants to hire a potential murderer to solve their mysteries. And I still haven't been able to crack that missing pet case. It just hasn't been a good week." He sighed, gingerly sipping his steaming coffee.

"I'm sorry. I haven't seen any sign of the dogs either; if I do, you'll be the first to know." She paused, considering her next words. She didn't want him to know that she had spoken to Detective Jefferson; surely that would go against his wishes of her not getting involved in the case, and he didn't need any stress right now.

"You know, I don't think anyone really thinks that you did it," she said at last. "They just don't have anything to point them towards anyone else."

"I wish I could be investigating this myself," he said with a frustrated groan. "But I'm afraid that it would just end up looking more suspicious to the police. Oh, I almost forgot, I did find out something interesting."

He took a moment to dig a folder out of the leather bag that he kept his files in. He pulled a paper out and slid it across the table to her. It took Moira a moment to figure out what she was seeing. It was a newspaper clipping from a few years ago. She recognized the face in the picture; it was the balding man that had been at the retirement party, and who had later come into the deli for a bowl of soup: Shawn Dietz. According to the article, he had been arrested for an armed robbery... and the lead detective on the case was Fitzgerald.

"Oh, wow," she breathed. "Did he escape from prison?"

"No, he served his time and was released early for good behavior. It seems like he came back here once he was free," David said. "He would definitely have motive to kill Fitzgerald, though. And I'm sure that he would have had the opportunity to learn a lot about killing from the people that he met in prison."

"Did you show this to the police?" she asked, pushing the paper back towards him.

"I did, but if they ever did anything with it, I never heard about it." He folded the newspaper clipping in half and slid it carefully back into the folder. "I guess I'll just have to wait and trust that the truth will come out. I'm glad that you believe me, at least."

Moira blushed, glad that he couldn't read her mind. Just a couple of nights ago she had been entertaining the thought that he might actually be the killer.

"I'm sorry, David," she said. "If there was any way that I could help you, I would."

He responded with a wry smile, "I know. Thank you, Moira. It means a lot to me."

CHAPTER ELEVEN

How to help David? The thought was on her mind as she drove back to the deli. She didn't know where the police were in their investigation, but they would certainly be wanting to make an arrest pretty soon. She knew that physical evidence would trump circumstantial evidence, and that even if Detective Jefferson thought that the private investigator didn't do it, he wouldn't be able to stop whoever else was working on the investigation from bringing him in.

The question was, was Jefferson convinced of David's innocence strongly enough that he would be willing to help her figure out who the real killer was? She didn't know, but she thought it was worth a try. She was sure that between the two of them and

David, they would be able to remember something from the night that Fitzgerald died that would point towards a different suspect. That Shawn Dietz guy might be a good place to start. Like David had said, the man had motive. He had been in prison for nearly ten years thanks to the brave police detective. All that she had to do was find physical evidence that he had something to do with Fitzgerald's death... or get him to confess.

Making a split-second decision, she turned into the police station's parking lot on her way back to the deli. If she was going to talk to Detective Jefferson, it might as well be now, when David's tired face was fresh on her mind.

"Ms. Darling, to what do I owe this pleasure?" the detective asked when he saw her. She was sitting on an uncomfortably hard bench in the police station's reception area, waiting silently while the secretary typed busily away on the computer.

"It's about David," she told him. "Can we go to your office?"

He led the way back through the police station. Moira was glad when they walked by the depressingly bare room where she had been interviewed when she was a suspect in the murder of a competitor. It was much more comfortable talking in Detective Jefferson's office, with his nice wooden desk, the picture of his wife and young children, and sunlight streaming in through the window. The room smelled of coffee, and he offered her a cup, but she shook her head, the taste of the coffee shop's overly sweet cappuccino lingering on her tongue.

"So, what is this about, Ms. Darling?" he asked once he was seated behind the wide desk.

"Please, call me Moira," she said. Maple Creek was a small town, and she saw the detective often enough these days that the continual formality felt weird to her.

"Very well, Moira it is." He leaned back in his seat and sighed. She realized for the first time that this investigation wasn't easy for him, either. He was trying to find the murderer of his partner—a man that he had looked up to and worked with for years —and all of the evidence pointed towards a man that he believed to be innocent.

"I just wanted to ask if you had anything—any leads at all—that point away from David," she said. "This is so hard on him. He's losing work because people think that he's a murderer."

"I don't have anything," the detective admitted with a sigh. He leaned back in his chair, staring at the ceiling. "No evidence that someone else was there, but no real evidence that *he* was there either, other than his wallet."

"What about that guy who just got out of prison?" she asked. "Shawn Dietz. He was in prison for ten years thanks to Detective Fitzgerald. Wouldn't that be motive?"

"Sure, it's motive," the young detective said. "But plenty of people would have had motive to kill Fitzgerald. He was a good detective, and was responsible for a lot of arrests. I read Dietz's file, and he was on his best behavior during his entire sentence. The armed robbery was his first offense, and he pled guilty. There were a lot of people involved in that case, and none of the others have turned up dead. The man has a good job with an auto repair shop, and from what his parole officer says, even got back together with his fiancée. He doesn't exactly sound like someone who was holding a grudge."

"And there's nothing tying him to the crime scene?"

Moira asked desperately. She knew that she was grasping at straws. "Nothing at all?"

"Not that I'm supposed to be telling you this, but no," the detective said. "There isn't."

She sighed, knowing that the detective probably couldn't tell her anything else. She had probably already overstayed her welcome; she shouldn't push it. She was just so frustrated; there was no way that David could have committed the murder, but it seemed like she was the only one who really believed that. Detective Jefferson said that he thought the private investigator was innocent, but he was still prepared to arrest David if the evidence continued to point towards him.

"Thanks for your time," she said at last, feeling defeated. She wondered if she had accomplished anything with this visit, other than learning that David's situation seemed even more hopeless than she had thought. "I should be getting back to the deli."

"I'm sorry that I don't have better news for you," he said, rising to walk her out. "I don't like this situation any more than you do. If there's anything that you can remember about that night, don't hesitate to give

me a call. I want to find the guy who killed my partner, and put him behind bars for the rest of his life."

Her mood was testy by the time she got back to the
deli. She did her best not to take it out on her
employees, but knew she was being short with them.
The whole situation with David was just so frighten-
ing. Part of her wanted to trust that the police
wouldn't arrest an innocent man, but she had
watched enough crime shows to know that it did
happen, more often than she had thought. What if
David ended up getting sent to prison for a murder
he didn't commit? He didn't deserve any of this, and
as far as she was concerned, the police were just
wasting their time trying to tie him to the crime.

Adding to her crankiness was her concern for her
daughter. Thankfully, the young woman was smart,
hardworking, and optimistic. Moira hoped that
Candice's positive outlook would help her achieve
her dreams, but she knew that a large percentage of
small businesses failed in their first year. They both
would be happier if Candice were able to secure the
space she loved—the little toy shop that was meant
to be closing— however, they still hadn't heard from
Henry, David's elderly friend who owned the place.
David continued assuring them that Henry would

turn up soon, but Moira had recently noticed his concern whenever they talked about his friend. The old man was a fishing enthusiast and often took off alone to his cabin up north for weeks on end, but he always told his friends when he left and when he was supposed to be back. This time, his vacation had been unexpected and no one was sure when it would end.

She let Dante and Darrin get to work on cleaning out the pantry in the back—somehow the spices always got disorganized, no matter how neatly she tried to keep them—while she cleaned the glass display cases up front. Once those were sparkling, she started on the floor. She began to calm down as she mopped, telling herself that she was being ridiculous and overreacting. *Jefferson wouldn't let them arrest the wrong man*, she told herself. *He wouldn't want the person who really committed the crime to walk free.* Plus, if matters got worse, David would hire a lawyer. She was sure that he would be able to find a good one; he was bound to have met quite a few in the course of his job.

And as for Candice, well, no matter what happened she could always count on her mother to have a place for her in her home and at the deli. Moira would do all that she could to support her daughter, and even if her dreams of opening a candy shop never came to fruition, at least the young woman would have a warm home and a steady job to fall back on.

The deli owner leaned on her mop and gazed at the now clean floor. She felt better, having expended much of her angry energy in her cleaning efforts. The deli looked pretty good now, too. Maybe she should be upset more often; she always seemed more inclined to clean when something was bothering her.

Motion outside of the deli's front window caught her eye, and she looked up to see her friend Martha walking across the parking lot with a gorgeous fluffy collie in tow. Moira stared at the dog for a moment and, wishing that she had the paper with the photos of the missing dogs, rushed out the front door to meet her friend.

CHAPTER TWELVE

"Isn't she beautiful?" Martha said, stroking the dog's soft head. "I was so alone in that big house without Emilia. Now I'll have someone to take care of again."

"She is very pretty," Moira agreed. "Where did you get her?" She wasn't an expert by any means, but she was almost certain that it was one of the missing dogs that David was trying to find. How would she tell her friend that her new pet was probably stolen?

"I saw someone selling her in a parking lot," the other woman said. "The man said that she didn't get along with his other dog, and that he just wanted her to go to a good home. She was only a hundred dollars, and she's purebred."

Moira bent down to get a better look at the dog. She squinted at the collar, hoping that whoever had stolen her hadn't been smart enough to remove the tags, but no such luck. She reached out to pet the silky fur, and then stood back up. Martha looked so happy, and the deli owner felt bad for what she was about to say, but she knew that there was probably someone out there that really was missing the dog,

"I hate to say this," she began. "But David's working on a case right now involving stolen dogs... and one of them was a collie." Martha's eyes widened, and her happy expression fell away.

"Oh dear, you don't think this sweetheart was stolen, do you?" She looked down at the dog sadly. "If she was, I'll do the right thing and give her back, but she's such a sweetheart. I'm going to be heartbroken to see her go."

"I can't tell if she's the same dog as the stolen one or not, but David has pictures of all of the missing dogs. Would you be willing to wait here while I call him?" Her friend nodded, so Moira held the door open for them and invited both woman and dog inside. "Just keep her away from the meat," she said. "I don't think my customers would be too happy to find dog slobber on their groceries."

She stepped back behind the register to grab her phone, and speed dialed David's number. He answered quickly, and she told him what had happened. He promised to be right over, and Moira turned back to her friend. Martha was stroking the dog, her face sad.

"Do you remember what the seller looked like?" she asked,

"Not really," her friend admitted. "He was maybe a decade younger than us, and he was wearing a gray sweatshirt."

"Do you think that you'd recognize him if you saw him again?"

"I guess." Martha shrugged. "My focus was on this sweet girl." She patted the dog, who licked her hand. "Not on the person getting rid of her."

Moira turned her phone's screen back on and flipped through the pictures until she found the ones that she had taken off the hooded man walking the poodle and the beagle.

She handed the phone to her friend.

"I know these aren't the best pictures," she said. "But do you recognize anything about this guy?" Martha gazed at the photos for a moment, then nodded.

"I'm pretty sure that it's the same person. I think the guy I got my girl from was wearing the same shoes, and he had a beagle in the back of his truck."

"Do you remember anything else about him? Could you describe his face? Did he give you his name?" The deli owner leaned forward, staring hopefully at her friend. She was disappointed when Martha shook her head.

"No, sorry, he didn't give me his name, and like I said, I wasn't really paying much attention to what he looked like."

Moira sighed, wishing that she had more to go on, but still feeling certain that the man her friend had gotten her dog from had been the thief. If only she had a way to identify him other than his shoes.

"Do you want a bowl of soup or anything?" she asked at last. "David's coming from Lake Marion, so he'll probably be about twenty minutes."

Two bowls of soup and a grilled chicken breast for the dog later, David's familiar black car pulled into the deli's parking lot. He hurried inside, and then froze, staring at the dog. Pulling a picture out of his wallet, he compared it to the pooch.

"Carrie?" he said. The dog pricked up her ears and wagged her tail at him, recognizing the name. David grinned.

"It's her," he announced, turning to Moira. "It's the stolen collie."

Moira knew that it was good news; with everything that was going on in David's life right now, a break in the case that he was working on was bound to be a relief. However, she couldn't help but feel sad at the crushed look on her friend's face.

"I'm so sorry," she said, walking to Martha and giving the other woman a hug.

"It's okay. It's good that her family will be able to get her back," her friend said. "I hope that you catch the guy that stole her in the first place. Stealing people's pets and reselling them is just a cold-hearted thing to do." She paused, then continued, "but getting a dog is a really good idea. I'll have to check out the shelter tomorrow."

"We'll catch him," David promised. "Now, tell me exactly where you met him."

David left shortly after with Carrie the collie in tow. He planned to return her to her owners straight away. They were probably frantic with worry about her; she seemed like such a sweet, well-cared-for dog that Moira couldn't imagine her not being loved. At least one of the missing pets would have a happy ending. She could only hope for such a good outcome for the others.

CHAPTER THIRTEEN

The private investigator drove away from the small country house on the outskirts of Lake Marion with a glad heart. The collie's family had been overjoyed to see her, and the pooch had returned the sentiment, jumping up and down eagerly as her people greeted her. He had refused payment; it felt good to do a good deed, and besides, the case still wasn't over. The other dogs and the thief were still out there, somewhere.

He decided to drive by the parking lot where Martha had picked up the dog. He followed her directions to a small, deserted lot near the grocery store in Maple Creek. It seemed as good a place to start looking for clues as any, but he hadn't really expected to find anything majorly helpful. He was surprised to see activity in the far corner of the parking lot; someone was standing next to a pickup truck, chatting intently on his cell phone. There were a couple of plastic kennels in the back of the truck, but David was at the wrong angle to see whether they had dogs in them.

His heart pounding, the private investigator coasted into the lot. He drove slowly towards the truck, doing his best to be prepared for anything. If the man really was the thief, there was no telling how he would react if he thought he was going to be caught. He could do anything from pulling out a gun to jumping in the truck and peeling away.

David got close enough to see that a couple of the kennels did have residents. He recognized the brown face and droopy ears of a beagle, and knew that he had found the right guy—or at least, the right dogs. There was still a chance that this man wasn't the dog thief, but was a partner or accomplice.

"Excuse me," he said, rolling down his window as his car pulled even with the truck. "Do you know where the closest gas station is?" He of course already knew exactly where every gas station was for miles around, but he wanted an excuse to talk to the man, to see his face and hear his voice. Anything that would help identify him later.

To his surprise, the man seemed to recognize him. When he looked into David's face, his eyes widened, and his mouth parted in shock. He hung up the phone without saying goodbye to whoever was on the other line, then pointed down the road.

"That way," he said quickly. "Just keep going, you'll see it." The man was pointing him in the opposite direction from the gas station. Intrigued, David nodded a quick thanks and rolled up his window. He pretended to follow the man's directions, pulling out of the parking lot and rounding the corner, but turned his vehicle around at the first intersection. He idled at the stop sign, the parking lot and the man's truck just barely in view. When the truck pulled out of the parking lot and drove in the opposite direction down Main Street, David followed, already on the phone with the Maple Creek police station.

CHAPTER FOURTEEN

Moira pulled into the parking lot of the Redwood Grill, feeling bad that she was slightly late. Yesterday, David had caught the man responsible for the rash of dognappings in the area, and tonight they were going to celebrate. It seemed like things were finally looking up again for the private investigator, and hopefully soon all of the stolen dogs would be reunited with their owners.

"He's in the back. You know the way," the hostess said with a smile, recognizing Moira instantly. She thanked the young woman, and slipped past the line of people waiting for seating. Sure enough, David was seated at their usual table. He had already ordered a glass of wine for both of them, and was perusing the appetizer menu while he waited for her.

"Sorry I'm late," she said as she slid into the booth across from him. "The kitchen sink at the deli got clogged and flooded, and I had to stay late to make sure it got cleaned up."

"Don't worry about it," he said, offering her a grin. "I've just been looking at their new menus. Denise wanted to see what I thought. Well, she wanted *your* opinion on them, but since you weren't here yet, she decided mine would do."

"I'm sure whoever she hired to design them did a great job," Moira said. "That woman doesn't cut corners." She took a sip of her wine, pleased that David had thought to order a glass for her. "So, have you had any luck figuring out who that jerk sold the stolen dogs to?"

"Not yet." David grimaced. "From what I've heard, he's not cooperating with the police. He's refusing to say anything without his lawyer, so they're holding him until his public defender arrives."

"Did you find out anything about *why* he was stealing the dogs? What's his name, anyway?" she asked.

"His name is Mikey Strauss, and from what I gathered he's not admitting to *anything* right now. He said that the dogs in the truck were his, and that he had to find them new homes because his landlord said he had too many." He sighed and took another sip of his wine. "He's not making this easy for any of us, but if your friend Martha can pick him out of a lineup, then things should go more smoothly."

"She'll be more than happy to do that, I'm sure. She was pretty upset that she bought a stolen dog." Moira lowered her voice and glanced around to make sure no one was nearby listening in. "Has there been any more news about the other case?"

She didn't have to elaborate; he knew immediately what she was talking about. David's expression darkened, and he put down his wine glass.

"No," he said. "Not that I've heard. But everyone at the Maple Creek police department seems to think that I did it. You should have seen some of the looks I got when I came in with Strauss."

"I'm sure they'll find another lead eventually," she told him. "And even if they don't, they don't have enough to arrest you on. The only evidence that they have that really points towards you being the murderer is the fact that your wallet was found in Fitzgerald's house. I already told Detective Jefferson that you'd lost it the night we had dinner, and once they check with your credit card company and your bank, they'll see that you reported it missing days before the murder. I just wonder how it ended up at the crime scene?"

"I've got no idea. Most likely, I dropped it outside while I was arguing with Fitzgerald. Maybe he picked it up and meant to return it to me the next day, and then forgot about it," David suggested.

"What was that argument about, anyway?" Moira asked, still curious about what would have caused the normally calm private investigator to lose his temper, and with a police detective of all people.

"It wasn't anything important," he said, looking away. "Do you know what you want to order?"

Why won't he just tell me? Moira wondered. *What could be so bad that he won't say it?* Neither David nor the detective were unreasonable men, and she couldn't imagine what would cause them to argue, especially in such a public setting.

"I think I'm going to go with the mushroom-stuffed chicken breasts today," she told him, deciding once again not to press the matter. "How about you?"

They were only a couple of bites into the main course when David's cell phone rang. He ignored it at first, muting the call and cutting a bite from the juicy steak on the plate in front of him. When it rang again, he sighed and gave in, shooting Moira an apologetic look as he answered it. She gave him a quick smile to let him know that it was okay—both of them were dedicated to their jobs, and that meant being available twenty-four hours a day. She took another bite of her chicken, savoring the rich, smoky cheese flavor of the creamy mushroom filling.

"I have to go," David said when he hung up. He dug into his new wallet and put some bills on the table. Moira looked up at him, concerned. Had something gone wrong with one of his cases?

"What's going on?" she asked.

"They want me down at the police station," he told her. "They said they have some questions to ask me.

115

You should finish up here. Visit with Denise." He gave her a small half smile. "I'm sure it's just about the dog thief." Moira couldn't help noticing how worried he looked as he walked away.

David walked into the police station, going over his brief telephone conversation with the detective. Nothing had been said to indicate that he was in any sort of trouble, but he had picked up on something off in the detective's tone. Why was he being asked to come to the station so late in the evening? Surely anything to do with the dog thief could wait until tomorrow.

"David Morris," he told the woman behind the counter at the police station "I'm here to see Detective Jefferson."

"I'll let him know," she said. "Have a seat." He obediently went to sit in one of the uncomfortable plastic chairs, but had barely reached the seat when a door opened and Jefferson poked his head out.

"David," he said. "Thanks for coming down to the station. Come with me."

He followed the detective down the familiar halls, and was surprised when they stopped in front of the suspect interview room instead of continuing to Jefferson's office. What was going on? Had the dog thief decided to talk before his lawyer got there? If so, why would they need him there? Usually, once David turned a criminal in to the police, the matter was out of his hands. He wasn't involved with the investigation past that point at all. So, what was going on here?

"Right in here, if you will," the detective said. David preceded him through the door. Instead of seeing Mikey Strauss sitting at the table in the center of the room, there was a uniformed officer standing in the corner. There were only two plain metal chairs in the room, one on each side of the table. David sat in the one on the far side from the officer, and Jefferson sat across from him. He looked sad, which scared David more than anything.

"Do you know why you're here?" the detective asked.

"No," David said honestly. "I thought at first that it must be something to do with the Strauss guy that got arrested yesterday, but I'm beginning to think that it doesn't have anything to do with that."

"Well, you're mostly right about that," Jefferson said. "This is a much more serious matter than someone selling stolen dogs." He took a deep breath. "Let's go over the night of the retirement party again, David."

"What do you want to know?" He felt sick. Enough time had passed since the murder for him to start hoping either that the police had found another suspect or had decided that they didn't have enough evidence against him. It looked like he had been wrong.

"Where were you that evening?"

"I was at the party, with Moira. I'm sure other people saw me there too. We already talked about this—"

"I just want to make sure that I'm getting the facts straight, David," the detective said. "Bear with me. Now, we both know that you arrived at the party later in the evening than Moira did. Can you tell me where you were before that?"

"I was at the office, working on a case."

"Can anyone verify that?"

"No." David sighed. He'd told the detective all of this already, and his answers weren't going to change.

"What route did you take when you were driving from your office to the party?"

"Um, I'm not sure," he replied, thrown for a moment. This was new. "I took Main Street to Greene, I think, and then parked on the street." The detective scribbled a note.

"Do you remember what you were wearing that night?" Another new question. Where was the detective going with this?

"Ah… a black duster, black jeans, and a dark green button-down shirt, I think." He only remembered because he had changed at the office right before meeting Moira at Fitzgerald's retirement party. He had spilled coffee on his other clothes earlier in the day, and hadn't wanted to show up to the party stained and smelling like a cappuccino.

"When we interviewed you last week, you were favoring your arm. Do you remember how you injured it?"

"A biking accident. I've been trying to exercise more regularly lately." He had already answered this question, too. Why was Jefferson going over all of this again? "Would you mind telling me what's going on?" he asked the detective. "Am I being held here, or am I free to leave?"

"I hate to say this, David, but I'm going to have to hold you here overnight." The young detective sighed and, with a weary expression, gestured to the officer in the corner. "You're being placed under arrest for the murder of Detective Fitzgerald. You have the right to remain silent..."

Jefferson's voice faded away as David sat back in shock. Under arrest? For murder? His mind was numb, and he almost didn't believe it—until he felt the cold steel of the handcuffs tightening around his wrists.

CHAPTER FIFTEEN

David's car was still in the parking lot when Moira pulled into the station. She hadn't let herself worry too much when he left the restaurant to answer questions for the police, but when he hadn't called her by the time she got home, she had started to worry. How long could it take to answer a few questions? She had decided to drive by the station, telling herself that she could stop at the grocery store on the way back—she and Candice were almost out of coffee at the house, which was an emergency in its own right.

Now she wasn't sure what to do. If David was still answering questions, she wouldn't want to interrupt him. But what if something else was going on? He had looked worried after the call at the restaurant, and she hadn't been able to get his expression out of her mind. She would go in, she decided. Just to make sure everything was all right.

Someone was already speaking to the woman behind the bulletproof glass at the counter, so Moira took a seat. She had been in this building so often in the last few months that she felt like she knew it almost as well as she knew the deli. A quick glance at the small stack of magazines showed her that there weren't any new issues to browse through, so she began fiddling with her phone, doing her best to not listen in to the argument taking place only a few feet in front of her.

"But I need my truck," said the man at the counter.

"It's been impounded, sir. I'm sorry, but the impound lot won't be open until eight o'clock tomorrow morning."

"Well, how do you expect me to get home?" The man was getting belligerent.

"I can call a taxi service, or you can call a friend or family member for a ride."

"Great," the man snarled. "Call the darn taxi. Tell them I need to go to Pineview Apartments, building number three. This totally sucks. When will I get my truck back?"

"You'll have to pick it up from impound in the morning."

"Fine. This is totally screwing me up."

The man grabbed a plastic bag containing a few personal items and turned towards the door. Moira barely held back a gasp when she saw his face. It was the man with the spiky hair—though the gelled spikes were drooping now—that had been rude to her at the deli. What was he doing here? Something about his outfit looked familiar, but it took her a second to place the gray sweatshirt and the sneakers. When she realized who this man must be, it was all that she could do not to exclaim out loud. This must be the dog thief.

Moira kept her eyes on him until he left the building, then stood on shaky legs and, still trying to make sense of what was going on, approached the woman behind the glass. She knew that she wouldn't have any luck asking about the man that had just left, but maybe she could at least find out where David was. She wondered if he knew that the guy that he had nabbed had just walked out of the building.

"Hi," she said to the woman. "Um, I'm Moira Darling. I'm just wondering if David Morris is still here?"

"Just a second, dear," the woman said. She typed something into the computer, asked Moira to spell his last name—which she did—and then typed again. "He's here, but he isn't allowed visitors for twenty-four hours," she said. "Unless you're his lawyer. Are you his lawyer?" She squinted at the deli owner over her glasses, assessing how lawyerly she looked.

"Visitors?" Moira asked, confused. Realization dawned slowly. "Wait, he hasn't been arrested, has he?" The woman nodded.

"Sorry, hon. Are you a relation?"

"No." She felt faint. What had happened? Why had David been arrested, and the thief had walked free? "If I can't see him, can I at least see Detective Jefferson?"

"I'll page him. Have a seat, honey. You look pale."

A few minutes later, Detective Jefferson walked into the room. He looked exhausted, and not at all surprised to see her.

"Come on back," he said. "Do you want a coffee?" She realized how late it was; the detective must be running on fumes.

"I shouldn't," she said. "I'll be up all night. Thanks for the offer, though."

They walked back through the station to his office. For the first time, Moira wondered where the holding cells were. What were they like? Was David comfortable?

"I know why you're here," he said as he shut the office door behind them. "And I don't think I can help you, but I'll answer questions if I can."

"Why did you arrest him?" she asked. "I thought you didn't believe that he was the killer."

"I don't know what I believe." The detective sat down heavily in his leather chair. "All I know is that, legally, I have enough evidence linking him to the crime to hold him for forty-eight hours. I need that time to figure some things out."

"How can you have evidence linking him to something that he didn't do?" Moira asked.

"There was a witness, Moira," Jefferson said in a dull voice. "Someone that saw him leaving Fitzgerald's home the night that he was killed."

This news stunned her, sent her reeling as her mind tried to take it in. A witness? But David would have told her if he had been at Fitzgerald's house that night, wouldn't he have?

"What if the witness is lying?" she said after a moment.

"He could be," the detective acknowledged. "But he was able to correctly describe the coat that David was wearing that night. David corroborated it himself."

"David almost always wears the same coat," Moira said. "That doesn't mean anything. He loves his duster. Who was the witness?"

"You know I can't tell you that," Jefferson said with a grimace. "I really shouldn't be discussing any of this with you, but I absolutely cannot give out any personal information."

She barely heard him, because her mind was already spinning. It was starting to make sense; the guy that got arrested because of David's investigative work just walked free, while the private investigator himself was in jail.

"It was the dog thief, wasn't it?" she asked. "That Mikey Strauss guy." Detective Jefferson didn't say anything, just stared at her. *If only I could remember where I saw him before,* she thought. She was almost certain that the deli hadn't been the first time she'd seen him. She closed her eyes, digging through her memories, and then suddenly got it. She *had* seen him before he had come into the deli to buy soup. He had been one of the onlookers during the argument between David and Detective Fitzgerald outside the Redwood Grill. The only question was why would he lie about seeing David come out of Fitzgerald's house? Even if she didn't firmly believe that the private investigator was innocent, she would be suspicious of such a large coincidence.

"Thanks for talking to me," she told Detective Jefferson. "I'll be back tomorrow to visit David." She gave him a weak smile before rising to leave. There was something she had to check.

The Redwood Grill was so dark when she pulled into the parking lot that she was worried that no one would be there. She was relieved to see a car sitting at the edge of the parking lot; at least the building wouldn't be completely empty. It was later than she had thought, but this really couldn't wait until morning. Not with David's freedom on the line. She crossed her fingers, and was rewarded with even more good luck when Denise answered her pounding at the door.

"Moira?" the red-headed woman said, gazing at her friend in surprise. "What is it?"

"I need to see your security footage from two weeks ago," Moira said. "Do you still have it?"

"All of our footage is stored for twelve weeks," the restaurant owner explained. "But why do you need to see it?"

"It's David. He's in jail, and the police think he murdered someone, but I might be able to prove that he didn't." It was a rushed explanation, but luckily the other woman seemed to accept it.

"What cameras do you need to see footage from?" she asked. Moira glanced up at the two video cameras hidden just above the restaurant's front door on the outside.

"Those," she said, pointing up.

"Follow me, we can watch it in my office."

It took them a few tries to find the right date, but when they did, they found the argument between the two men easily enough. It was an odd experience to watch the encounter on a small monitor through a fisheye lens. Moira felt guilty, like she was invading David's privacy, but she knew that if her hunch was right, this might be the only way to free him.

"It doesn't do audio," Denise said apologetically.

"That's fine," she replied, hoping that her blush wouldn't show up in the dim lighting from the TV's screen. She tried to tell herself that she wouldn't want to listen to the argument anyway. If David didn't want to tell her, that was his right and she shouldn't try to find out what it was about behind his back. "I just need to see something..."

She paused and rewound the video, leaning forward to peer at the screen. She thought that she had seen something fall out of David's pocket... *there*. A small, square black shape fell out of his coat pocket as he gestured angrily. That must have been his wallet. She let the video play for a few seconds longer, watching herself come out of the restaurant and the two men stop arguing. Both looked embarrassed, she could tell by their postures. What on earth had they been talking about? Why did they both stop so suddenly when she came through the door?

The video continued to play, showing them walk away. A few more seconds passed, and then someone stepped into view from the side. She recognized his spiky hairdo immediately, even though he was wearing a different shirt than he had been wearing today. Mikey Strauss. He bent down and picked up David's wallet. He rifled through it, and she saw him pocket the cash before he walked away, David's wallet still in his hand.

CHAPTER SIXTEEN

"Detective Jefferson, please. It's Moira Darling, the detective and I spoke earlier tonight," she said, trying to keep her voice calm. She was sitting in her car in the dark parking lot of the Redwood Grill. It had started to rain, and the water drummed on the roof of the car. She usually found the sound comforting, but right now the added distraction was just irritating.

"He just left," came the woman's voice. "Can I take a message?" Moira bit back a groan of frustration.

"It's an emergency. Can I have his personal number?" she asked.

"We can't give out that information. Can't this wait until tomorrow? It's very late. If it's a real emergency, you should hang up and call nine-one-one."

"Please," the deli owner said desperately. "It's not that sort of emergency, but I need to talk to him right now. If you can't give me his number, can you call him for me?"

"Oh, all right. I'll call him and give him the message." The dispatcher sighed. "Give me a moment to pull it up."

Moira drummed her fingers on the steering wheel as she waited. She was relieved when Detective Jefferson called her back almost immediately. She quickly explained what she had discovered and waited for him to process the information.

"If what you're saying is true, then I just let my partner's murderer walk out the door of the police station," he said quietly. "Do you have a copy of the video?"

"Denise emailed me the footage," she told him. "I can forward it to you."

"Please do. I'll need to review it, and go over a few things at the police station," he said. "If you're right, we may have this in the bag by tomorrow."

"You're not going to arrest him until tomorrow?" Moira asked, shocked. "What if he escapes? He could be leaving town right now."

"There's a process to these things. I can't just go arresting whoever I feel like. I want the real murderer in jail just as much as you do, but I have to follow procedure. I don't know how long all of this will take." He paused. "Go home, Moira. Get some sleep. I'll give you a call tomorrow, or David will when we release him. Thank you for your help." He hung up, leaving Moira with a silent phone pressed against her ear.

There is no way I'm going to be able to get any sleep tonight, she thought as his ridiculous advice echoed in her ears. *Not with David in jail and the real murderer free to disappear.* But what more could she do? Bothering the police wouldn't do any good. Detective Jefferson had already been far nicer to her than he had needed to be, and although it was frustrating that he couldn't just rush over and arrest Mikey

Strauss on her say-so, it was a good thing that he was following procedure.

She started her car and pulled out of the parking lot. She meant to go home, but her foot seemed to stall on the gas pedal as she approached the intersection in the center of town. She couldn't stand the thought of the spiky-haired dog thief slipping away in the middle of the night. If he left, then Jefferson might never be able to see his partner's killer behind bars, and it might be harder for David to clear his name. *If all I do is watch his apartment*, she thought, *what's the worst that can happen?* She knew from overhearing his conversation with the woman at the police station that he was staying with a friend at Pineview Apartments, which was only a couple of minutes away. If she just parked in the lot and kept an eye on his friend's building, she would be able to tail him if he tried leaving. It seemed like something that David would do, and after all that he had done to help her, she owed it to him to make sure that the guy that had falsely accused him didn't get away. Her phone was halfway charged, which should be enough to last her through the night at least.

She debated about whether or not to tell Candice what she was doing, and decided against it. Her daughter was probably already asleep, and would likely try to convince her mother that staking out a murderer alone was a bad idea.

The apartment complex was easy enough to find. The hard part was choosing a spot to park. Thanks to the rain, visibility wasn't that good, and she had to be close enough to see the entrance without her car being too obvious. She settled on a spot a row away from the sidewalk, shut her headlights off, and slid an audio book disc into the CD player. This was definitely better than tossing and turning in bed at home, if a bit less comfortable.

She was just beginning to get bored sitting in the car when she saw a large dark shape come hurrying around the side of the apartment building. It was a dog, unleashed and sopping wet from the rain. It sniffed at the corner of the building for a moment, and then darted into the parking lot. Moira stared at it, unsure what to do. It could just be a stray, or it might be one of the stolen dogs. She couldn't very well let someone's missing pet wander around in the rain, could she? With a sigh, she broke her promise to herself not to leave the car, and opened the driver's side door. She would just see if the dog was friendly, that was it. If it seemed lost, she could let it into the back of the car, and she'd take it to the shelter in the morning.

"Here, doggy," she called softly. The rain was lightening up a bit, and her jacket sufficed to keep her from getting too wet. "Where'd you go?"

The dog appeared between two cars, startling her. This close, she could see that it was a German Shepherd, a big one, with more black than tan. She had never been nervous around dogs, but she found herself hoping that this one wasn't a biter.

"Hey, sweetie, are you lost?" she asked. She held out a hand, and the dog stared at her for a moment before moving a few hesitant steps closer. He looked a bit on the thin side, but didn't have the mangy look of a stray. A thick black collar wrapped around his neck, but she couldn't see any tags attached to it.

Were any of the stolen dogs German shepherds? she wondered. She didn't think that any on the original list had been, but David had said that more dogs had gone missing.

"Are you stolen, buddy?" she asked, crouching down in an attempt to appear less threatening. The dog seemed to appreciate the gesture——he walked over and sniffed at her hand, then wagged his tail as she petted him. *I wish I could call David,* she thought. She didn't know what to do now that she had made friends with the dog. If it was one of the stolen dogs, then she couldn't just leave it here. But if it was somebody's pet that had slipped out for a midnight stroll, then she didn't want to cart the pooch all the way to the animal shelter.

"There you are," a sharp voice said, startling both her and the dog. "Bad boy, Maverick. Get over here."

Moira looked up and her heart faltered when she saw the owner of the voice. It was the man with the spiky hair, Mikey Strauss, striding around the corner of the building with a lit cigarette in his mouth. *So much for my stakeout,* she thought. *What do I do now?* There was no way that the man hadn't seen her—she was crouched in the middle of a parking lot, petting the dog that he was talking to. Thunder rumbled in the sky as he approached. Moira withdrew her hand from the dog's fur and rose slowly.

"Come here, I said." Strauss's voice was angry, and when he gestured with the hand that was holding the cigarette, the dog flinched and trembled, pressing himself into Moira's leg. "Sorry," he said grudgingly, glancing at Moira. "He usually listens—" He froze, the cigarette dropping from his hand and falling to the ground to sizzle out in a puddle.

"It's you," he said. She took a step back. "You were at the police station. And at the deli." He frowned. "You were at that restaurant too, weren't you?" He took a step forward, his eyes dark and full of suspicion. "Are you following me?"

"No," she said in a trembling voice. "I'm not. I—I just..." she trailed off, unable to come up with a good explanation. She took another step back, wishing that she hadn't moved quite so far from her car to find the dog.

"Why would you be following me?" he mused. He snapped his fingers and the dog finally slunk towards him, tail tucked between his legs. "I don't like it when people follow me."

She backed up a few more steps, eager to put as much distance between them as she could.

"I'm not following you, I promise."

"I think you are." His gaze narrowed. "Are you working with the police?"

"No, I'm not." She hoped that he would hear the ring of truth in her voice. She most definitely was not working with the police at the moment. In fact, they would probably be pretty unhappy if they knew she was there.

To her relief he didn't say anything else, just stood there frowning at her. She was beginning to think that she would be able to get away, when her cell phone rang. Mikey's gaze snapped to her pocket.

"Who is it?" he asked. She hesitated. He lunged forward, quickly closing the distance between them. Grabbing her arm and holding it away, he dug into her pocket, removing her keys and dropping them carelessly to the ground, finally reaching her phone. He looked at the screen. Moira glanced at it too, and was surprised to see David's name on the caller ID. Had he been released from police custody?

Mikey mouthed the name, his face furrowed in concentration. She could tell that he recognized David's name, and she saw the exact moment that he made the connection. His face paled, and he tossed her phone to the ground.

"You're coming with me," he growled. "I get the feeling that I'm going to need a bargaining chip." He reached for her arm again, but Moira twisted out of the way and ran blindly for the car. She was expecting to feel him tackle her at any moment, but instead heard a splash followed by a stream of curses, and then a yelp. She couldn't risk a look over her shoulder to see what was happening, but hoped that the dog was all right.

The second she reached her car, she yanked the driver's side door open and got in, then jabbed her finger at the lock button. She heard the click of all four doors locking just as Mikey reached the vehicle. He pounded on the window, his pale face twisted in anger. All Moira could do was sit there and stare at him as the rain began to fall harder, and the wind picked up.

CHAPTER SEVENTEEN

When Mikey walked away, Moira breathed a sigh of relief. She thought that he was giving up, that he had realized that there was no way to reach her. As soon as he disappeared from sight, she would leap out of the car and make a dash for the fallen keys. Then she would get out of there and head straight for the nearest pay phone.

But the dog thief didn't go in the building. Instead, he walked up to a station wagon, opened the trunk and rummaged around in the darkness. When his upper half reappeared, he was holding a long crowbar. Moira let out a squeak of fear and looked around the car for anything she could use to defend herself. There was nothing. She was a tidy person, and didn't even have a spare coffee mug in her car, let alone anything that could be used as a real weapon.

She watched with terror as the man approached. He twirled the crowbar with an ease that gave her shivers, and from the expression on his face she could tell that he was enjoying this immensely.

Realizing that her only hope of escape would be if she could outrun him, Moira struggled into the back seat of her car, giving herself easier access to the rear doors. As soon as he broke a window, she would escape out the opposite side and run as far and as fast as she could.

Her plan was good in theory, but she wasn't prepared for how casually and quickly the man acted. He approached her car and, as soon as he was in range, swung the crowbar at her front windshield. It didn't shatter quite like she had expected, thanks to the safety glass, but with his second hit, most of the glass caved in.

Moira screamed as he walked around to the driver's side and did the same thing to the front window.

Run, she told herself, but her body didn't seem to be listening to her brain at the moment.

It wasn't until he was approaching the back window that her survival instinct kicked into gear and she slid to the other side of the car, manually unlocked the door, and threw herself into the downpour. She heard his footsteps rounding the car, and knew that he would be on her in moments.

She wasn't the fastest runner at the best of times, but tonight she felt like she was moving in a dream. No matter how hard she pounded her legs, she felt like she was moving in slow motion. Mikey's shape loomed behind her, and out of the corner of her eye she saw him raise the crowbar. He might not have originally planned to kill, but in the thrill of the chase, he seemed to have forgotten his desire for a hostage.

Moira squeezed her eyes shut and tried her best to duck the blow. She knew that she hadn't been fast enough, and was prepared to feel the sharp pain of the blow.

A sudden loud *snap* shocked her, and she had just enough time to throw her hands out in front of her to cushion her fall before she smashed into the ground. Her ankle blazed with pain, and she realized that one of her heels, which she had worn to dinner with David earlier in the evening, must have broken. A moment later, Mikey, unable to stop his momentum, tumbled over her. She heard a sharp clang as the crowbar landed only inches from her head.

Struggling to untangle herself, Moira managed to get to her feet. Mentally cursing her choice in shoes, she reached down and tried to snap off the remaining heel like she had seen people do in movies. Either they used special prop shoes, or she was even more out of shape than she had thought, for all she accomplished was scraping the palm of her hand.

Mikey was beginning to reach for the crowbar so, left with no other choice, she began to hobble away from him. Between the unevenness of having one three-inch-high heel and one broken one, and the flaming pain in her ankle, her pace was slow, but the dog thief must have been injured in the fall as well, because he was still on the ground, a groan coming from his lips.

Moira was heading back to her car—the windows might be broken, but if she could find the keys, it would still drive—when she saw flashing lights on the main road. She paused, hoping, and felt almost faint with relief as the police car turned into the parking lot.

CHAPTER EIGHTEEN

"David's coming over," Moira told her daughter from the couch. "He said that he'll be here in a few minutes."

"All right, I'll go make sure the door is unlocked." Candice paused at the entrance to the living room. "Are you sure you don't need me to get you anything else?"

"I'm fine for now, sweetie," she replied. "Thanks." She gave her daughter a grateful smile and rearranged herself on the cushion, then winced when her ankle began throbbing. She knew that she was lucky to escape last night's fiasco with nothing more than a sprained ankle and some scrapes, but being injured was never fun.

"How are you doing?" David asked when he got there. He looked tired, but happier than he had in a while, besides the concern for her that pulled his brow together into a slight frown.

"I've been better," she said. "But I've also been worse. It's not too bad. I'm supposed to take a couple of days off." She made a face, and he laughed.

"Anyone else would be glad to have a few days of guilt-free bed rest, but not you," he said fondly. More seriously, he added, "I'm glad you're okay."

"Thanks. Me too." She smiled at him. "It's good to see you. I'm so glad they released you as soon as they realized the truth."

"Detective Jefferson is a fair man, and he cares about getting the right guy. He was very apologetic when he let me out of the cell."

"It's good that he was so quick to review the evidence," she said. "Otherwise you might have had to spend the whole night in the holding cell."

"And you might have been Mikey Strauss's next victim." David's frown deepened, and he sat down on the chair across the room from the couch. "You need to stop getting into trouble, Moira. The stress of worrying about you is going to be the death of me."

"It's not my fault. I think I'm cursed," she joked.

"You definitely lead quite the life for someone who runs a deli."

"Not by choice." She sat the rest of the way up, trying to think through the pain. "So, why did Strauss kill Detective Fitzgerald?" she asked. "Was it just a coincidence?"

"No. It was premeditated. Several years in the planning, in fact." David sighed. "Five years ago, Fitzgerald arrested Mikey Strauss's father—his only family. Strauss Senior got life with no chance of parole for a double homicide. This was a revenge killing."

"Wow." She sat back, leaning against the couch cushions. "I would almost feel bad for Mikey, if he weren't a murderer, of course. Why did he try to frame you? Did you have something to do with sending his father to prison?"

"No, I think my involvement was just bad luck on my part. He must have realized that with the public argument and my wallet as evidence, I would be a pretty convincing suspect. I don't think he was planning on staying around for too much longer. He had a big stack of cash in his friend's apartment, likely from selling the stolen pets and pawning some stuff he'd stolen," he said.

"Speaking of the argument," she began.

"I'll tell you what it was about," David said, surprising her. "But I don't want you to get upset."

"I can't promise that until I know what it was about," she pointed out.

"Of course you can't," he said, the ghost of a smile appearing on his lips. "It was about you."

"Me?" she asked.

"Fitzgerald made a comment to me about how he wished that you would keep your nose out of police business. He thinks you're deliberately putting yourself in harm's way. Apparently, he thought we are... um... closer than we really are. He told me that I should be able to keep a tighter rein on 'my woman,' and that he'd rather you stayed home altogether."

As Moira gaped in shock, David continued with a grimace, "I couldn't just let that pass. Any of it. So, I told him that it wasn't my place to keep you anywhere—that you were a free agent and could handle yourself. That even if we were... um... closer, that you were perfectly capable of making your own decisions and maybe you wouldn't have to get so involved with solving crimes if he was better at his own job. Which, as you can imagine, he didn't like very much."

Moira was stunned. Her emotions were mixed; part of her was hurt that the detective had thought so little of her. It wasn't like she sought out murderers and thieves. On the contrary, it seemed like she couldn't avoid them. She was also touched that David would defend her, and speak up on her behalf even when she wasn't around.

"Thank you," she said at last. "For telling me, and for defending my honor."

"You're welcome." He grinned at her. "One more thing before I let you rest. Do you still want to get a dog?"

"Yeah, I do," she said. "I think it's time to open up my heart to another pet, and I don't think I'd be able to stand living completely alone when Candice leaves."

"Wait here." Moira gave a snort of unladylike laughter—as if she was going anywhere with her sprained ankle. A moment later, David came back. To her surprise, Maverick the German shepherd was trailing behind him on a leash. As he saw Moira, Maverick rushed forward and put his head on her lap.

"Couldn't you find his family?" she asked, leaning forward and petting the dog.

"He wasn't stolen. He belongs—belonged—to Mikey Strauss," David explained. "Strauss relinquished him voluntarily when his friend began telling Jefferson about how Mikey treated the dog. He's yours if you want him. Otherwise, he'll probably find his way to a rescue group of some sort." He gave the dog a fond look. "This guy saved your life, you know."

"He did?" Moira asked. "How?"

"According to Strauss, he tripped over the dog when he started chasing you." David smirked. "He fell into a puddle. He was more upset about ruining his cell phone than losing the dog."

Moira remembered the sounds of the dog thief falling and the dog yelping. She stroked Maverick's soft fur, and knew that she didn't need any time to think about it.

"Of course I'll keep him," she said. "He'll have a home here for the rest of his life."

AUTHOR'S NOTE

I'd love to hear your thoughts on my books, the storylines, and anything else that you'd like to comment on—reader feedback is very important to me. My contact information, along with some other helpful links, is listed on the next page. If you'd like to be on my list of "folks to contact" with updates, release and sales notifications, etc.... just shoot me an email and let me know. Thanks for reading!

Also...

... if you're looking for more great reads, Summer Prescott Books publishes several popular series by outstanding Cozy Mystery authors.

CONTACT SUMMER PRESCOTT
BOOKS PUBLISHING

Twitter: @summerprescottı

Bookbub: https://www.bookbub.com/authors/ summer-prescott

Blog and Book Catalog: http://summerprescottbooks.com

Email: summer.prescott.cozies@gmail.com

YouTube: https://www.youtube.com/channel/ UCngKNUkDdWuQ5k7-Vkfrp6A

And...be sure to check out the Summer Prescott Cozy Mysteries fan page and Summer Prescott Books Publishing Page on Facebook – let's be friends!

To download a free book, and sign up for our fun and exciting newsletter, which will give you opportunities to win prizes and swag, enter contests, and be the first to know about New Releases, click here: http://summerprescottbooks.com

Made in the USA
Monee, IL
31 May 2022

97275880R00089